LORDS OF THE EARTH

DAVID BOWLES

SEVERED PRESS
HOBART TASMANIA

LORDS OF THE EARTH

www.severedpress.com

ISBN: 978-1-925493-85-6

PROLOGUE: POPOCATEPETL

Popocatepetl had reverted to relative calm after the eruptions of 2016, but CENAPRED, the National Center for Disaster Prevention, continued its constant vigil of the volcano, aided in these telemetric observations by the Mexican Secretariat of the Interior and experts from the National Autonomous University of Mexico (UNAM), as well as the collaboration of the US Geological Survey's Cascades Volcano Observatory.

A week before the First Emergence, all fifteen stations on the slopes of Popocatepetl began to detect seismic activity as well as a spike in the levels of SO_2 and CO_2. The telemetry, analyzed by CENAPRED's processing hub, triggered a series of automated messages to private cell phones and email addresses. Within the hour, the Scientific and Technical Advisory Committee—made up of researchers from UNAM and CENAPRED—met to review more than fifty telemetric signals. The committee immediately recommended the government institute a phase-3 yellow alert and evacuate a radius of twenty kilometers.

The decision saved thousands of lives, a relatively small comfort given the millions of deaths to come.

For four days, nearby Mexico City and Puebla experienced a tremor or two every twelve hours, the shocks hovering around 2.5 in magnitude. Then, on the morning of the fifth day, Popocatepetl erupted violently with the force of 18 megatons of TNT, sending a column of ash fifteen kilometers into the air and a wave of lava—the pyroclastic flow—rushing down the slopes at 300 km/h.

Everything in a ten-kilometer radius was obliterated. For another fifteen kilometers beyond that, trees and structures were cropped close to the ground. Mere minutes after the eruption, the entire Izta-Popo Zoquiapan National Park had been laid waste, and several nearby towns were scorched and shattered.

As the plume spread tephra into the stratosphere over the next eight hours, it triggered torrents of volcanic ash rain through which lightning jagged ferociously, kindling fires among felled trees throughout the park.

Beneath the ugly bruise of the sky, relief efforts began in the seared zone around the blast area, and prevailing winds off the Gulf pushed the ash toward Mexico City, where fifteen centimeters soon coated cars and streets, exacerbating the accustomed smog and causing multiple deaths from respiratory failure and collisions. The day after the eruption, the sun never shone on the capital. During that ominously long night, citizens were urged to remain indoors at all costs. Private automobiles were prohibited from circulating.

The seventh day after Popocatepetl's quickening, the flow of magma suddenly ceased. To investigate, a CENAPRED technician named Julio Quintero Flores guided a drone over the smoking caldera. Its camera captured something truly inexplicable.

Buoyed by black slag was a huge ovoid stone, two hundred meters from tip to tip.

The director general of CENAPRED, Miguel Ramos Zepeda, immediately reconvened the Scientific and Technical Advisory Committee, and initial hypotheses were put forth in a barrage of data-driven speculation as members drew on their own expertise and robust webs of research connections.

None of them could have possibly guessed at the truth.

At 7:49 a.m. on the third day since the explosion, as the committee watched in silent horror, the massive stone split like a cocoon. Wedging themselves into the crack came six sapphire talons the length of pickup trucks, glinting in the half-light as they slowly pried the ellipsoid open. Then, through that gaping crack, something unspeakably massive clawed its way out into the pumice-choked, steaming air.

The drone caught a quick glance at a white-hot impassive eye before the signal went dead.

CHAPTER ONE: ELENA

For Elena, it was as if her very heart had been wrapped in a funeral shroud. The oppression of the ashy darkness triggered horrible memories, experiences that she normally kept at bay with work or drink. The city shrank until it was the confines of a closet, the strange men just outside the door, laughing as she cried, gagging her when she screamed.

Her voice had not been strong enough to save her as a child. As a woman—respected scientist, author, TV host—she strove with every passing day to remedy that weakness. Yet Don Goyo (as she and her colleagues lovingly referred to Popocatepetl, living embodiment of Mesoamerican grief) had burst his heart at last, plunging the central highlands of Mexico into bereft black. She once again felt trapped, cut off, enervated.

The short blast of a horn sounded faintly, cutting through the gloom.

"No rest for the wicked," she muttered to no one, shaking off the doldrums as she slid her tablet into her bag. Dropping a broad hat onto her loose brown curls, she locked the door to her condominium and headed for the elevator.

A car from Canal 22 was waiting for her at the curb just outside her apartment building. The driver inclined his head toward her as he opened the back door, a handkerchief clapped to his mouth against the ash.

"Morning, Dr. Baz," he said, his eyes crinkling with a hidden smile. "Weather sucks, doesn't it?"

"Pretty much, Juan, yeah." She slid into the seat, taking her hat off and shaking the ash off onto the sidewalk. "That's what happens with plinian eruptions, even a VEI 4 like this one."

He squinted. "I'd ask what the hell all that means, but I guess I'll just wait for your show this Sunday."

"Every viewer counts," she quipped, arching an eyebrow.

"Well, there'll be no show if we don't get moving. Watch your foot."

Soon he was behind the wheel and they were headed to Churubusco Studios, just a short distance from Elena's home in the Country Club neighborhood of Mexico City's Coyoacán borough. On one of the smaller soundstages, her weekly science program *Muñecos Cósmicos* was filmed for broadcast on Canal 22, a channel managed by the Secretariat of Culture. When she had taken over hosting duties three years earlier, the series had been tottering on the verge of cancellation—several misguided studio changes had reduced it to the worst sort of pseudoscientific pabulum. Elena, with her government contacts, had fought to bring empirical rigor back to the show without destroying its quirky sense of fun. Part of that transformation had been moving production out of the station facilities to this more cutting-edge studio, nestled in the sprawling complex that now loomed in the half-light like a besieged castle.

The streets were mostly empty, save for a few pedestrians with medical masks, and the gloomy parking lot seemed like the set of some post-apocalyptic horror film, replete with cars on which volcanic ash had settled like nuclear winter. Protecting herself as best as she could with her hat, Elena made her way inside. No sooner had she cleared security when her assistant Ramona approached, tablet in hand, an accustomed look of hurried concerned stamped on her features.

"Eddie wants to talk to you," the younger woman said breathlessly, reaching out to brush ash off her boss's shoulders. "He made changes to your changes."

"Typical," Elena muttered with chagrin, handing Ramona her bag and hat before heading to find the show's producer. She had known Edgardo Santayana Creel since childhood—they had both attended Colegio Williams, one of the best private schools in

Mexico City. He was a talented businessman with a sharp, creative mind.

He was also a sneaky little bastard.

"Alright, Eddie," she sighed when she found him near craft service, sipping coffee. "What didn't you like about my changes?"

"Not dramatic enough. The eruption is a massive story, the biggest in decades. People will be tuning into this episode like they never have before, Elena. It'll be a ratings landslide. The tweaks you made on the science are fine, all that stuff about the sonic boom and so forth, but I want to stress the dangers. The graphics department is working on some truly epic animation to go along with the video clips, and I need you to—"

She arched an eyebrow. "Doesn't all this strike you as being in really bad taste, given the rising death toll from people who ignored the evacuation order? Changing the episode at the last minute to explore the science behind volcanoes? That makes sense. But you're pushing the limits of decency, Eddie."

"Casualties. Exactly. Don't you get it? We have an obligation to share worse-case scenarios with people, Elena. That way they'll stop ignoring government instructions. We're saving lives."

Giving a half-hearted laugh, Elena shook her head incredulously. "You're so full of shit, Eddie. Fine. Leave in my additions, and I'll read your weak exercise in theatrics."

He smiled. "Deal. Now go get yourself prepped. Sandra's meeting with the camera guys, but she's anxious to start shooting already."

At make-up, Diego clicked his tongue at her as he picked ash from her hair and blouse. "Doc, really? You're pale enough without coating yourself with a layer of grey. Ah, well. Nothing that some strategic rouge can't fix."

While he went to work on her, Elena closed her eyes and reviewed key points from the script. The words would scroll through a teleprompter, of course, but she'd found that she came off much more natural if she essentially had her talk memorized. She preferred not to loop anything in ADR if she could help it, not beyond the voice-overs required to narrate animation and video.

"Elena?"

It was Sandra Rivera Katz, the director for most of this season's episodes, frizzy hair pulled loosely back in a ponytail.

"Hey."

"So it looks like we might have to film the third segment before the second. Your guest has been delayed by an electrical storm."

Diego pulled away the bib protecting her blouse, and Elena stood, nodding. "No problem. Ready when you are."

Sandra hesitated a moment, looking down at the physicist's right hand. "Um, Elena?"

"What?"

"Can you take off the glove?"

Annoyed, feeling that old powerlessness creeping in at the edge of things, Elena flexed the fingers of her prosthetic. "It's ridiculous, you know. What matters is my knowledge. That's what they're tuning in for."

"Come on, don't be naïve. You get the fan mail. You know they love to see your myoelectric hand. You're the 'cybernetic scientist' to millions of viewers, Elena. I know it feels exploitative, but you can't accept their adulation on your own stuffy terms. That's not the way this works."

Cybernetic scientist. It wasn't the only nickname people had for her. But Sandra's larger point was well taken—she *had* sought the limelight, after all. Along with her eager work as a consultant to the military, it had given power to her voice, had lessened her sense of weakness. Her words and ideas were wielded on the national and international stage to combat many ills. The scales were by no means balanced, but it was a start.

The price, of course, was this objectification, this othering of her disability. At the end of the day, however, she preferred that dull ache to the impotence of her childhood memories.

"Fine," she grunted, thrusting her sleeve up past her elbow and rolling down the silicon sheath that covered her military-grade prosthesis, all glittering black and silver. "If they want *Star Wars*, that's what we'll give them."

Ramona swooped in from seemingly nowhere to take the glove, and Elena followed the director to the soundstage.

Technicians fitted her with a lapel mic, and she sipped water while everyone ran through a systems check.

Sandra signaled everyone to silence, and then cameras began to roll.

"Good evening, friends. It's a black day for Mexico, but science is a candle in the dark. Today on *Muñecos Cósmicos*, we'll be discussing the eruption of Don Goyo and its repercussions for our country. I'm your host, Elena Baz Dresch." Here, she reached out her metal and carbon hand to the camera, beckoning gently. "Won't you walk with me on the edge of Occam's Razor?"

"Jesus Christ!" someone shouted.

"Cut!" Sandra called. "Quiet on the set! Who the hell was that?"

The gaffer was gesturing at his smartphone. Other members of the crew had begun to cluster around him.

"It's Amecameca. Somebody's streaming live. There's a ... a freaking *monster* wrecking the city."

Sandra scoffed. "No time for bullshit hoaxes, people. We have a show to film!"

One of the technicians switched the large monitor in the back to a news feed, catching a newscaster mid-sentence.

"... smashing houses underfoot, its tail digging enormous furrows in the earth. We go now live to our reporter Samuel Amador at the Amecameca city plaza."

The image switched to a distressed man standing before the arch that led into the plaza. In the distance rose the charred and glowing slopes of Popocatepetl. As Amador spoke, the camera panned away to something that appeared larger—a lumbering behemoth obscured by drizzle and ash.

"I'm here in the heart of this vacation spot. Fortunately, most of the population was evacuated before or immediately after the volcano's eruption, because ... though it seems crazy to say it ... the city is under attack by an enormous creature."

Lightning cracked overhead, illuminating the monstrosity for a moment. It was covered with a rough, jagged carapace that scintillated with impossible hues of blue in the brief light. Elena could make out two staggeringly huge legs that towered as high as the Monument to Independence in downtown Mexico City.

Before she could contemplate the thing's vastness further, the camera operator zoomed in on the Parish of the Assumption just as an enormous claw reached down and scooped it out of the ground, hefting the former monastery into the air and heaving it into the distance. Jerking and shaking, the camera followed the trajectory of pink stone as it shuddered apart mid-flight and went smashing into a distant part of the city.

Then there was a view of the ground as the camera operator began to run.

The news feed plugged in several other views of the destruction, live streams from social media and the like. The monstrosity's tail, which appeared to end in talons or pinchers, flicked against the colonial-era arch. A smartphone caught the image of the medallion of Humbled Christ set in the keystone, cracking and exploding outward as the sandstone disintegrated.

The newscaster's voice cut in, shaky and breathless.

"For those just tuning in, about forty-five minutes ago, something enormous emerged from the caldera of Popocatepetl. After making its way down the lava flows, it headed for the city of Amecameca, to which it is presently laying waste."

Diego gasped. "That's only a freaking hour away!"

Sounds of explosions and gunfire rattled the speakers. The television camera operator and field reporter had found a safer vantage point, and the screen now showed multiple impacts against the behemoth as arriving military began to pound it with mortar, rockets, and other projectiles. Elena recognized a dozen ERC-90 armored cars as they burst into the plaza, their 90-millimeter canon hurtling shell after shell.

The monstrosity shuddered under this barrage, bending over to present its awful face to the soldiers. White eyes like blazing suns peered from over a long, serrated jaw like that of a prehistoric crocodile. With a single almost dismissive motion, it swept the armored cars aside, sending them tumbling among the rubble in its wake.

The gargantuan thing took few more lumbering steps, and the newscaster began to speculate.

"The creature appears to be heading toward Sacromonte Hill, where…" a pause as someone muttered in his earpiece "…the Sanctuary of the Lord of Sacromonte was erected during colonial times over an ancient Aztec shrine."

The behemoth slammed its claws into the hill and ascended quickly. From its silhouette against the slope, Elena judged it to be nearly 150 meters tall.

Impossible.

Nonetheless, the vast torso soon towered over the old church. That long jaw opened wide, and another, blunter snout—flashing blue-white and slimy with every flash of lightning—pushed forward and vomited a flood of iridescent bile that burst into flame as it hit the air and rained down on the sanctuary like napalm, reducing the buildings to slag in a matter of seconds.

The silence in the studio was absolute. Everyone stared at the screen, stunned. What could be said? What could be done?

In that quiet, Elena heard her phone ring, playing the theme to Carl Sagan's *Cosmos*. Those sparse notes by Vangelis echoed ominously throughout the studio. She heard Sandra sob softly.

Ramona rushed toward Elena, clutching the phone like a holy relic.

"Dr. Baz, it's for you. Urgent, he says."

Elena took the phone in her myoelectric hand without thinking. The grip adjusted with a few twitches of her bicep.

"Who?"

"General Quiroga."

Nodding, Elena lifted the phone to her ear.

"Marco. Let me guess. You want my help stopping it."

CHAPTER TWO: ALFONSO

Alfonso Becerra Cruz pulled his headphones off at last, nodding as he scrolled back up through his proposal. He'd been working for nearly eighteen hours straight, shutting out the world with music, deliberately turning off his internet router and smartphone in order to resist the temptation to waste time with trivialities. He was aided in his focus by the perpetual gloom from Popocatepetl's explosion, though he'd had to turn up the volume several times in the last two hours as a few slight tremors had spawned shrill sirens. This was Mexico City, after all. He knew the drill. It would take more than an uneasy metropolis to distract him.

His seclusion was not the idiosyncratic tic of a quirky archeologist. Alfonso had learned the hard way, putting himself through college while working a full-time job and moonlighting in restaurants as a mariachi singer—distractions sapped his intellectual energy. During crunch time, he removed himself from the world completely. And today definitely qualified as crunch time. It was vital that the Council of Archeology from the National Institute of Anthropology and History approve his proposed dig near Toluca, where he had recently discovered evidence that Olmec influence had spread even further into the highlands than Zazacatla.

But he was thankfully done with the bulk of the work. Now he just needed to shunt the documents to his fellow researchers for whatever final tweaks they might want to make.

Stretching till his joints popped, Alfonso yawned and nodded at the painting of the Olmec dragon deity that hung on the wall opposite his desk. Then he stood, his fingers lightly brushing a statue of the world tree that a Maya artisan had carved for him out of ceiba during his time in Quintana Roo. The bird at its apex— the very tip of the flowered, reptilian tail—looked up at him expectantly.

Yes, I know, Itzamna. Time to reconnect to the virtual world.

As he walked over to the router and flipped its switch, something hoarse and violent rattled the windows of his apartment.

Another storm, he thought. *Volcanic ash disturbing the atmosphere. Crazy lightning and thunder. Freaking internet had better work.*

It didn't.

"Son of a bitch!" he muttered, fumbling around for a USB drive and shoving it into a free port on his laptop. As the files were sluggishly copied onto it, Alfonso powered his phone back up.

He had 57 missed calls.

"What the hell?"

His laptop dinged, and he yanked the USB drive free. Sliding it into his breast pocket, he grabbed his keys and an umbrella. He was going to have to brave the ash and rain to trot a block down Iztaccihuatl Avenue to the cybercafé. Perhaps he'd even find a taxi braving the strange weather that could drop him off at the National Institute of Anthropology and History itself, which wasn't that far, after all. His little apartment in the Condesa neighborhood of Mexico City's Cuauhtémoc borough cost him almost half of his salary, but it was worth it to live just a few minutes from crucial spots like the National Museum of Anthropology and Chapultepec Park. Even the Templo Mayor, the great pyramid of ancient Tenochtitlan, was only a half hour away.

As he opened the door, he lifted the phone to his ear to listen to the most recent message. It was from his ex-wife.

"Goddamn it, Alfonso, turn your phone on! We're watching this insanity on TV, and Ramiro is scared out of his mind. You can't do this to your son, idiot. You need to let him know you're okay."

Alfonso shook his head as he locked the door and turned to step into the street. *Crazy broad. It's just some ash and lightning.*

A whistling groan filled the air, a sound like bombs falling.

Alfonso pivoted toward movement that he glimpsed out of the corner of his eye.

A bright red Metrobus came screaming out of the sky at impossible speeds. Alfonso jumped back just as the rapid transit vehicle slammed into the blacktop, ripping up huge chunks of asphalt and hurling them against buildings and cars as it bored into the street and then flipped over, completely crumpled and mangled. Body parts were flung free, landing up and down the block with gruesome, squelching thuds.

"What the …?"

A harrowing, cavernous snarl echoed deafeningly all around. Glancing up, Alfonso saw—high above the rooftops several blocks over—a massive and monstrous head moving along Insurgentes Avenue. Vaguely reptilian, it was covered in jagged, spiny chitin that continued down over what he could see of its torso. The uneven plating suddenly glinted blue as fire from a passing attack plane spat bright yet ineffective against that impossible flesh.

The plane wheeled through the sky, circling the invading behemoth and preparing for another barrage. But a great taloned fist came swinging in a perilous arc and batted the aircraft into a sprawling music store, where it exploded with a concussion that was quickly drowned out by the beast's bone-rattling howl.

Alfonso's phone buzzed in his hand. A text message. Opening the application with a trembling finger, he saw that there were dozens from friends, colleagues, relatives.

you okay, dad?

answer, dumbass!

condesa under attack! stay away from insurgentes!

reports say moving from coyoacan to cuauhtemoc so be safe!

if you're still in mexico city get the hell out now

amecameca razed to the ground!

seen this monster that came out of the volcano? remind you of something?

That message, one of the first to come through, was from a number he didn't recognize. There was an image attached, a photo of a ceramic figurine from Xochicalco with which Alfonso was very familiar.

The newest text was from a colleague, Ruth Garibay, whose initial work in Toluca was the basis for the new proposed dig. Alfonso stared at the picture she had attached for some thirty seconds before reading her note.

been sitting on this for a year worried about blowback—not the first one, Poncho.

His mind reeling, he reviewed the previous messages, which provided a patchwork of information that he wished he could confirm on news websites, but the passage of the behemoth and likely multiple calls for aid were overwhelming the nearby cell towers. From what he could piece together, however, the giant reptilian thing had emerged a few hours ago from a huge stone cocoon in Popocatepetl and had since made its way into Mexico City, razing everything in its path.

Alfonso's eyes glassed over as he stared at the wreckage in the street without registering the sheer carnage that the mangled steel and flesh hinted at. His mind was whirring.

Stone cocoon. Reptilian behemoth. Volcano.

"Oh, shit," he muttered aloud. "I think I know what this is."

Without another moment's hesitation, he turned southeast and began walking briskly along Iztaccihuatl, pulling up his son's number in his contacts. The boy luckily lived with his mother in Reynosa, right on the US border, but Teresa was right—it wasn't fair to let Ramiro worry. After a weak ring, he got an automated Telmex message about busy circuits, but he kept redialing with the phone on speaker. From time to time, he looked roughly north at the receding back of the beast, which appeared to be stomping its way toward Paseo de la Reforma.

Sirens grew louder as he crossed a deserted Campeche Street. Employees of the cybercafé had crowded outside of their building, staring up at the leviathan lumbering into the distance. The few other open businesses had similarly emptied into the ash-choked street, their fear fading to curious, spectating horror as the danger shifted to other parts of the capital. Alfonso threaded his way among their sober conversations and attempts to contact loved ones, not lingering or responding to questions. His need drove him to a trot as he cleared the throng.

On the sixth attempt, the phone kept ringing. A voice answered with hurried hope. "Dad?"

"Yes, son, it's me."

"Holy crap, Dad! There's a freaking monster in your neighborhood! I was so scared something had happened to you."

"Yeah, I saw it just now. But I'm fine. It's gone off toward the north."

Ramiro swallowed audibly. "North? Like, what, toward *us*?"

Alfonso realized his mistake. "No, kid, no way. Relax. It's very, very far away from you. Plus, the army's fighting it. You don't need to worry."

"Uh, we've been watching it on TV. The army is getting its ass kicked."

"Well, that's because they don't know what they're up against yet. But I'm…I've got some information that can help."

"Okay …" The boy sounded dubious. His mother had put too many negative ideas about his father's abilities for him to just buy into this notion. "Be careful, okay?"

"I will. Tell your mom not to worry."

"She's not. She's just pissed."

Sirens sounded keener and closer as he rounded the corner onto Insurgentes Avenue. The cratered prints of the creature had reduced much of the thoroughfare to a blasted battleground. Incongruously, between two vast depressions stood an intact eucalyptus tree, its branches shaken free of the ash that coated so much else.

"Alright, Ram, I need to go. I'll call you back soon. Promise."

"Okay. Love you, Dad."

"Me too, kid. Bye."

Disconnecting, Alfonso took stock. Up and down the avenue, broken cars and smashed buildings wreathed smoke into the darkling sky. The cries of the wounded could be heard even above the teams of emergency services, whose sirens wailed as they attempted to navigate the depressions and rubble. Craning his neck, he peered up at the INAH building that housed most of the administrative offices of the National Institute of Anthropology and History. To his relief, it was mostly intact, except for a taxi that had been shoved halfway through a tenth-floor window and the shattered ruins of a helicopter still burning on the roof.

Carefully circumventing a live wire that snaked angrily across the sidewalk, Alfonso crossed Aguascalientes Street just as some INAH personnel began trickling out in a shell-shocked daze. Catching sight of Pamela Chapa Fuentes, Subdirector of Studies and Projects, Alfonso hurried close.

"Pamela."

"Dr. Becerra? What the hell are you doing here? That thing could double back any minute, sir."

"I doubt it. Anyway, where's Francisco?"

"Excuse me?" She was glancing all about, overwhelmed by the devastation. "Oh, Mr. Vargas is still up in his office, trying to get through to the general director."

"Thanks. Be safe, ma'am."

Inside the buildings, the lights flickered so erratically that Alfonso immediately rejected the idea of taking an elevator. He rushed up the six flights of stairs as quickly as he could, heading straight into the office of the National Coordinator of Archaeological Projects.

Francisco Vargas Magar was nodding, phone cradled between cheek and shoulder, while he jotted notes down on a block of paper.

"Yes, sir. Understood. Like I said, I had managed to evacuate all but a skeleton crew before it got here, and now we're heading out, too. Yes, I imagine so. We could always use the back access. Only the tenth floor. Right. Okay. Keep me in the loop."

Hanging up, Francisco turned and saw Alfonso standing in the doorway.

"Ah, I should've known you'd come calling. Why couldn't your ass have rented an apartment on the other side of Mexico Park?"

"Nice to see you too, asshole."

They smiled at each other for a second.

"So, what can I do for you, Alfonso?"

"I need you to pull some strings, get me in contact with CENAPRED."

Francisco raised an eyebrow. "I'm guessing they're a little too busy to contend with archeology just now."

"Trust me, they need to hear this. It'll help them deal with this … monster."

Francisco dropped into his chair, rubbing his temples. "Man. Hrm. Alright. Let me think … okay. Here's the deal. General Marco Navarro is putting together a team of experts. I could probably get you in to see them, recommend you as a possible adviser or something."

Alfonso stepped toward his desk eagerly. "Yes! That's perfect, man."

"There's only one caveat, my friend. Guess who he's put in charge of the team? Your favorite bionic Barbie. The Cosmic Puppet herself."

Alfonso closed his eyes. "Of all the goddamn luck."

With a chuckle, Francisco picked up the phone.

"Oh, I'm sure you and Dr. Baz have a lot to catch up on. Haven't spoken much since that episode, huh?"

Alfonso shook his head and gave him the finger. "Whatever. Make the call. It's too important to let professional rivalry stand in the way. I can handle her. No worries."

Despite his bravado, the idea of facing Elena Baz Dresch again made his guts squirm in ways the threat of a gigantic reptilian leviathan simply couldn't.

CHAPTER THREE: MARCO

The bustle in the operational command module reached a fevered pitch as screens displayed multiple drone and satellite views of the hostile organism, plowing into Chapultepec Forest, the park at the heart of the capital. Division General Marco Navarro Alba, Commander of Mexico's First Military Region, gripped a technician's shoulder more tightly than he should as he leaned forward.

"Where are the goddamn jets?"

"En route, sir."

The President's voice—its normal silky smoothness now rough with anxiety and stress—rasped over the speakers. The hostile's present location was just minutes away from Los Pinos, the executive residence. Though secreted away in a bunker made to withstand a nuclear blast, the President and his cabinet were still very much at risk from the gargantuan invader.

"Are the tanks in place, General?"

As if summoned by their commander-in-chief's query, a half dozen ERC-90s came screeching to a halt in the ceremonial stone circle of the Altar to the Homeland. The vehicles' video feeds were shunted to the screens, and Marco watched as they began to pound the looming hostile with their cannon, filling the monument with smoke and fury.

The subterranean command module of SEDENA—the Secretariat of National Defense—from which the general was orchestrating the capital's defense, had linked up not only with the presidential bunker, but also with the city's state-of-the-art C4i4 Center, which managed control, command, communication, and computing for the municipality, as well as intelligence, investigation, information, and integration. The C4i4 technicians now piped in live video of three of Mexico's six F-5 jets screaming over Mexico City, converging on the hostile organism, which even now had reached the memorial to fallen military cadets and was crushing the armored ATVs. Wielding a blood-smeared vehicle between two gleaming talons, it sheared the tops off the six columns of the monument and opened its terrifying maw to loose an ear-splitting roar that overloaded the audio from the two drones hovering above it.

Marco turned to one of his colonels. "Weapons free, Rodolfo. Tell the fighters to blast the hell out of that thing!"

Within seconds, six Maverick missiles exploded against the hostile's armored hide, the intensity of the blast overriding all but satellite imagery for a few seconds.

"The bastard stopped its forward movement!" Secretary of National Defense Antonio Zepeda Aguirre crowed over the link to the presidential bunker. "Keep hammering it!"

In pretty quick succession, the F-5s wheeled about and landed another two rounds of missiles against the hostile, which was by this point visibly staggering under the attack. The jets followed up with low-yield cluster bombs and napalm before blasting at the organism with their guns as well.

As the flash and smoke cleared, Marco saw that the hostile was still standing, though it had completely halted and was writhing as if in pain or rage. Groans and expletives filled the room—the small telepresence screen nearby showed that the President and his cabinet were equally frustrated.

The hostile organism stopped shuddering and cocked its head skyward, glaring at a drone with a blazing white eye. Then it turned to Chapultepec Castle, spread majestic across the summit of a low hill where once the Mexica had made a last stand, and began lumbering toward the national treasure. With a few blows of fists, it reduced that museum to rubble before vomiting corrosion over the shattered stone, which sluggishly melted into flaming slag.

Snarling, the monster gazed to the northeast at the skyscrapers that glowed dully in the half-light. With a final blow to the hill from its tail, it headed out of the park, back into the city proper.

"Son of a bitch!" the President hissed over the link

An aid stepped close to Marco. "Sir, the team of experts is now set up in the conference room. The two from CENAPRED finally arrived just minutes ago."

Marco nodded and turned to the telepresence screen. "Mr. President, with your permission, we will now shunt your signal to the meeting with the emergency task force."

"Yes, General. And I'm sending you another member at the behest of the National Institute of Anthropology and History. Let's hope that between them, they generate some ideas we can use ASAP."

Turning to his colonel and the rest of the command staff, Marco swallowed heavily. "Do what you can to push it out of the city and into the mountains so that we can blast the hell out of it. Try to keep it from residential zones. Coordinate with C4i4 to ensure emergency services follow in its wake."

He slipped into the hallway that led to the conference room and pulled out his phone, hitting his wife's name in his contacts list. Both their phones were connected to the military intranet, so she answered almost immediately.

"Marco? Is everything okay?"

"Yes, within reason. I'm about to meet with some scientists who may give us an edge. Are you and the girls alright?"

"Sure, don't stress about it. The emergency facility is perfectly safe and comfortable, just as you said it would be. Susana and Olivia are spending time with the mayor's daughter. They know each other from college, apparently."

"Good, good. Just checking in. I'll keep you posted."

"Okay. I love you."

"Me, too. Good-bye."

Marco took a deep breath and strode into the conference room, slipping his phone back inside his jacket. A discussion faded to silence as he entered. Seated around the long table, amid a clutter of laptops and other devices, were the men and women who had been hand-picked for the team: astrophysicist Esteban Flores

Caballo, all crumpled clothes and smeared glasses; geologist Silvia Campa Sainz, steel-haired genius with an eternal bemused smile; biologist Astrid Estrada Corzo, deceptively young-looking Nobel nominee; and chemical engineer Roberto Menchaca Contreras, out-of-place among the other scientists in his black suit and tie.

At the head of the table, almost silhouetted by the glow of the monitors behind her, stood Elena Baz Dresch, her bionic hand clenched in a fist. Marco's chest tightened for a second as in his mind's eye her features became those of a terrified six year old, wounded and near death, whispering a ghastly but compelling command. The bond that joined them had lasted decades, had pushed Marco to protect his family more diligently than even his wildly zealous and macho father. But he could speak to no one else about that day, not even his wife.

To stop the flood of memories her presence always triggered, the general nodded briskly and addressed the group with gruff abruptness.

"I'm going to dispense with pleasantries. As Dr. Baz has no doubt told you in her briefing, I'm General Navarro." Picking up a remote, he activated the telepresence screen along one wall. "Joining us is the President and key members of his cabinet. We all understand the stakes. Right now, Mexico's in the midst of the most lethal crisis of its history. Of the world's history. We need answers fast. We need a response to this hostile organism before more citizens are killed, more patrimony destroyed."

"Understand," cut in the President, "the rest of the world is moving to aid us as quickly as possible. Just over three hours have passed since this thing emerged from Popocatepetl, but already US and Canadian troops are on the way. American aircraft carriers are redeploying. Jets are being scrambled to join in the fight. But I would prefer we defeated the hostile on our own, with Mexican brains and brawn."

Elena cleared her throat. "Well, you've got the best people for the job. Each of us is plugged into a network of experts that increase our knowledge and skill exponentially. We've begun some initial analyses that we'll share in a moment. The most important news is that we already have a possible weapon, Mr.

President. As you know, I'm one of several scientists that consult with the General Directorate of Military Industry of the Army. For the past three years, we've been developing a prototype cannon that uses sound waves to devastating effect."

The President glanced at the Secretary of National Defense. "Sound as a weapon? Does SEDENA agree that this is the way to go?"

Marco refrained from responding. Elena had sketched out her theory to the entire command staff, but the general had reservations about the environmental impact of the device.

Secretary Zepeda Aguirre nodded, however. "On the recommendation of General Navarro and the Center of Applied Research and Technology Development, I have set in motion the immediate deployment of the high-decibel ELF cannon developed under the guidance of Dr. Baz. Upon your authorization, we will use the weapon against the hostile once it has been lured or pushed from populated areas."

"And there's the rub," the President growled. "Look at the latest video. The thing has crossed Circuito Bicentenario and is heading up Paseo de la Reforma."

C4i4 was relaying images from traffic cams, ATMs, and building security surveillance. The hostile organism smashed through the overpass near United Nations Garden and looked up at the twin towers—Torre Mayor and Torre Reforma—both of which loomed some 100 meters over its fearsome head. Crouching, it beat its taloned fists into the asphalt, cracking holes into the infrastructure below, and then hurled itself with thundering steps at Torre Mayor, slamming its left shoulder against the skyscraper with awesome force.

Glass exploded outward in glittering torrents. The building buckled, swayed, but did not collapse.

Marco felt like throwing up. He had faced death and destruction before, but nothing could prepare even the most hardened veteran for such an apocalyptic scene.

"Tell me that goddamn tower was evacuated," gasped the President.

"Yes, sir." Marco realized he had whispered, and he stood straighter. "The last person was escorted out thirty minutes ago."

As if to show its indifference to such details, the hostile howled in apparent rage and began scaling the shuddering skyscraper, digging its claws deep into the steel as it jerked itself up toward the helipad at its summit. Another three F-5 jets boomed out of the ashen sky, sending sidewinders caroming into the monster's thick hide and the tower itself, which glowered orange-red from the explosions.

A fleet of Blackhawk helicopters joined the barrage, firing with everything they had, dropping small-yield bombs as they fluttered dangerously close to the invader. Suddenly, it pushed off the Torre Mayor, the force of its leap finally snapping the internal structure, sending the skyscraper collapsing into ruin as the hostile hurtled in a heavy arc between the twin towers. As it did so, its pincered tail seized a helicopter and flung it against one of the jets, brightening the artificial dusk with the glare of destruction. Arms spread wide as if to embrace, the organism landed on the upper half of the green-blue obelisk of the Torre Reforma, wrenching at its dizzying heights in an effort to fell it like a mortal enemy.

The monster started head-butting the building until it had ripped open a massive hole in the uppermost of its 57 floors. Then it vomited acid bile into the heart of the obelisk.

Jets continued to hurl missiles. Drones dropped napalm. But there was no stopping the inevitable.

Like a mighty tree, the Torre Reforma came falling slow. Its 246 meters bisected Pase de la Reforma at an angle, crashing into a third skyscraper, Torre BBVA Bancomer.

"Holy shit!" Roberto Menchaca muttered, aghast. "There goes the trinity of modern Mexican engineering."

Marco glanced at him. The chemical engineer had fear in his eyes.

Whistling in the dark. Wish I had the stomach for a little levity. But this bastard is tearing the guts out of my city. All I can do now is destroy it or despair.

Thudding away from the collapsing towers, the hostile kicked the Fountain of Diana the Hunter asunder without a moment's hesitation. The remaining jets had circled back around to drop what Marco suspected was their final round of explosives and missiles; they began to bombard the creature just as it reached the Angel of Independence, the winged emblem of the struggle for freedom perched atop its regal column.

As though it were a spear planted in the ground, the hostile seized the monument, ripped it free of its foundation, and hurled it at the incoming jets, which burst into flaming fragments that rained down against that blue-green armor with little apparent effect.

Elena gritted her teeth. "Enough. Enough, Mr. President. We understand what it can do. Shut off the feed, sir."

The screens went black, leaving just the telepresence monitor. Aids slipped pads and sheaves of paper into cabinet members' hands behind the President and Secretary of National Defense, both of whom were visibly shaken by what they had all witnessed.

"You see why we need the ELF cannon. Only extremely low frequencies have a chance of harming the hostile. Conventional weapons won't pierce that hide."

"Not hide," interjected Astrid Estrada. "A carapace of some sort. The organism itself is inside, protected by that chitin. Perhaps the ELF cannon will at the least damage it, leave a chink that the army can attack through."

Silvia Campa slipped her glasses off, bit thoughtfully on the frame. "If you're using ultrasound at high enough decibels, you might trigger localized tremors. Maybe even a limited earthquake."

Elena nodded. "We're aware of the hazards, which is why we need to get it far enough away from the city, into the mountains, before we attack it with the ELF cannon."

A voice from behind Marco interrupted. "Yeah, it's probably a bad idea to use that."

Elena's head snapped toward the door, and Marco's gaze followed hers. The compact, dark-complexioned man in the doorway was familiar looking.

Elena slapped her prosthetic hand against the table, palm down, hissing with disgust. "Jesus Christ, who let this clown in?"

The President's tone was cool and disapproving. "*I* did, Dr. Baz. This 'clown,' ladies and gentlemen, is Alfonso Becerra, notable archeologist and professor at UNAM. The general director of National Institute of Anthropology and History believes that Dr. Becerra has something extremely valuable to contribute to these efforts. Please, be accommodating."

Oh, great. Marco suddenly remembered the infamous episode of *Muñecos Cósmicos,* the media fallout from Elena's takedown of the archeologist.

Moving quickly to control the situation before her cold arrogance could recover, Marco addressed Becerra. "Bad idea to use the ELF cannon? Why?"

Becerra shrugged his backpack from his shoulder, set it on the table. "Because you'll wake up the others. This one's not alone."

Astrid leaned forward, dubious brows knitting together. "And, uh, how do you know there are more?"

"Because," Alfonso said in a matter-of-fact way clearly meant to hide his nerves, "I know what they are."

The entire table began speaking at once, and Alfonso dropped into a chair, lifting his hand as if he had the power to silence them. Amazingly, they stopped their incredulous harrumphing and listened.

"The creature that's presently making its disastrous way up Paseo de la Reforma? It's Xochitonal, an antediluvian demigod from Mesoamerican myth." Elena shook her head, turned away, but the archeologist plowed ahead breathlessly. "The Aztecs called it a *xiuhcoatl,* a fire wyrm. It belonged to group of titanic beings that once ruled the globe, according to the oldest sources. *Cemanahuaquehqueh.* Lords of the Earth."

CHAPTER FOUR: CHARLOTTE

August 10, 1938—

Last night, I dreamt of Father. We were on the boat, in the middle of Oneida Lake. I was young, perhaps eight years old, the age Mother finally relented and allowed me to accompany him during those long weekends upstate. Father had something on his hook, something heavy and determined. He was reeling the fish in, his rod bending sharply with the weight and struggle.

"Help me, Charlotte!" he cried. Though I didn't have his strength, I went to him, wrapped my small hands around the wooden grip of the pole, and began yank upwards and back as he reeled in our catch.

By degrees, it came up out of the water and over the starboard side of the boat, the hugest sturgeon I've ever imagined, taller than my present 5'2" frame, at least a hundred pounds of writhing flesh.

As it flopped on the deck, scales iridescent in the dawn, Father looked at me and smiled. "You're the greatest fisher in the world, little girl. Don't ever forget."

I woke up smiling and in tears. I'm sure that all the excitement about this year's Rio Grande Valley Fishing Rodeo has me so tense that even my dreams are trying to reassure me. Still, it was lovely to see the old man, even if in a fleeting vision of sleep. I do so miss him. The twenty years I spent with him off and on at Oneida and Onondaga molded me into the woman I am today. I know some people scoff behind my back, but James loves me despite my obsessions, and the three years of my marriage has shielded me against the worst of my withdrawals from family and New York lakes.

Not that South Texas lacks in great fishing. I still remember arriving at our sturdy new home in Bayview and finding that I could indulge my "hobby" out over saltier and broader waters. Starting with gulf trout and channel bass, robalo and salt-water pike, it didn't take me long to master the fine points of bay fishing. But those were small fry. The minute I heard of the fishing rodeo (still think it's a strange turn of phrase), I knew I could sweep the women's division. It didn't take much to convince James—he had been tempted to buy a yacht anyway. Soon, we were plying the Gulf waves aboard *Siren Spray*, Captain Phelps at the wheel. James was able to relax from the pressure of managing a chain of oil refineries—reading and sipping at drink or two—and I began to train.

Well, it sure paid off, didn't it? I found I had an uncanny sense for the denizens of the depths. Despite all the naysayers—those bulky, tough-looking women who raised their eyes at my slim frame and Yankee voice—I swept the women's division two years running. Last August, I boated a *7-foot-6-inch sailfish*. I have to admit: I took a certain selfish pride, seeing the egos of my competitors deflate as I was awarded the 200-dollar prize in front of one of the largest crowds ever to attend the ceremony.

But it's not enough. Call me arrogant, but this year I'm certain I can up the ante. Since we moved to San Benito, I've been out on the Gulf three to four days a week, preparing.

I'm going to gaff a blue marlin, the holy grail of deep-sea fishing. I'm going after the open championships, ready to show the men just what this little gal from Syracuse can do.

Just wait and see.

August 11, 1938—

Ah, it's been a long day, full of strange tales and cowardly men. I may have a sort of strange task before me. A quest, if you will.

I've written a little bit about the rumors and whisperings among Mexican fisherman this year. Ever since the Orizaba earthquake last year and the hurricane that followed it, there have been some very odd sightings down in the Bay of Campeche—an enormous leviathan, the gossip goes, parts of its bulk surfacing for brief seconds in the wakes of shrimping boats.

In recent months, the docks in Brownsville and Port Isabel have been abuzz with a new development: nets torn free from boats upon the Gulf waters just a few hours from our shores. I'll admit to being intrigued by the idea of some massive shark or whale, patrolling the depths, stealing the hard-won catch of unsuspecting men. But for the most part, I dismissed the gossip as a subset of fish tales.

This morning, however, when I went to continue stocking the *Siren Spray*, the marina was teeming with curious people. Today's edition of the *Brownsville Herald* features an interview with marine biologist Alton Hutson. Apparently, he's convinced that the creature is a whale shark, not a basking shark as some have been speculating. But as folks getting ready to compete confronted Mexican fisherman there on the docks, they kept hearing descriptions of the thing that conflict with both those theories.

Clara Thomas saw me trying to track down the latest news. "Whatever it is," she said confidentially, "lots of us are thinking about withdrawing from the rodeo, just to be on the safe side."

I wanted to laugh at this cowardice, but I just smirked instead. "Well, not me. And I'm betting most of the more serious fellows won't chicken out, either."

She looked at me curiously. "Well, you are a tough cookie, aren't you? Maybe you can join up with the foolish men who're thinking about organizing an expedition to catch it."

She was being ironic and mean-spirited, but I ignored the tone. "That's not a bad idea."

So I spent most of the next few hours approaching different competitors, getting a feel for which of them might be planning such a quest. Most, including the men, were visibly reluctant to even consider the idea. Finally, though, I bumped into B.B. Burnell, vice-president of the Port Isabel Chamber of Commerce.

"Oh, yeah, several of us are mulling it over, Mrs. Sewell. The *Andrey*'s a good candidate for flagship of the expedition, and I don't mind my cabin cruiser taking the lead. But you know how folks are. Big talk, but not much action."

"Well, I'm in. Sounds like an amazing adventure."

Burnell got this funny look on his face, and I knew what was coming. "I'm not sure it's a good idea for womenfolk to come along. Too much of a risk, you see."

He had more to say, but I just walked off, leaving him to spout his stupidity alone. As I reached the yacht, fuming inside, I was approached by a Caleb Jorgen, a reporter from the *Herald* who interviewed me last year after my win.

"Mrs. Sewell! Couple of quick questions if you don't mind."

"Okay. Shoot."

"What do you think about this supposed sea monster?"

"It's a potential threat to the coast and the fishing industry. Someone needs to get out there and hunt it down."

"There's talk of a search party. Would you be willing to join in?"

I laughed. "Of course I would. Problem is, the men around here are either too cowardly to start an expedition or too worried I'll show them up to invite me along."

"Yikes. You sound upset."

I took a deep breath, eased it out of my lungs. I thought of Father, imagined his wry smile as he winked at me. He had always indulged my whims, much to Mother's chagrin. He would back me up on this choice, too.

"I'll put it to you this way, Caleb. I'd like to catch the mysterious leviathan. If the men of Port Isabel aren't up to the challenge, well, maybe I'll organize something myself. Perhaps an all-women monster hunt."

His eyes went wide as he jotted down my quotes.

I can only imagine the shit-storm when the story hits the stands tomorrow.

Now I just have to figure out how to break the news to James. He has been terribly sweet and accommodating of my strange whims. But a monster hunt? He is going to be *very* pissed-off at me.

CHAPTER FIVE: ELENA

If it had been up to Elena, she would have thrown the fakir out of the conference room immediately. Too much was at stake for the team to spin their wheels in idiotic soft-science speculation. For a moment, adrenaline squeezed her heart like a vice as she thought of her own father's inaction, or rather his misplaced estimation of his power and cleverness. He'd refused to pay the ransom—the bastard—and the Hyenas had howled with mad laughter as they'd sharpened their machetes...

She whirled on Becerra, ready to pour her darkness out on him in a stream of cutting words, but the President spoke first:

"Interesting. For the moment, I'm going to approve the use of the, um, ELF cannon. While that initiative is underway, I expect this team to dig deep into one another's research and theories. Find out where this...*fire wyrm* is from. What are its weaknesses? I need auxiliary plans and an executive summary within the next few hours. General, we'll reconnect with you in the command module in fifteen minutes."

As Marco sketched a salute, Elena reached out and shut off the telepresence link.

"I need to talk to you, General."

He shot her a queer look and then nodded. "In the hall."

They stepped out of the conference room. The door clicked shut, and Elena leaned toward him in frustration.

"What the hell, Marco? Making me waste my time sifting through this joker's bullshit when lives are on the line?"

"Hey, I hear you. I didn't know who they were sending over, but *he's the President's guy*. I can't just yank him because you have bad history."

"It's not our history—which, uh, *what* history? One episode of my show? It's his complete lack of empiricism. Did you not just hear the crap he was spouting? Pre-Colombian demigods? Christ, Marco."

"Look, I'm no scientist, but come on. Hear him out. If you and the others decide—after careful consideration—that there's nothing to his ideas, I'll get the President to pull his ass out of here. In the meantime, *try to keep an open mind.* I've got to make sure your weapon is prepped and ready for transport."

Elena could only bring herself to make a grunt of agreement. Marco touched her arm, her right arm, with the slightest of reassuring gestures.

"I need you to manage this, El. There's no one I trust more than you to give us options. But I also know that darkness that's spilling out of your eyes. Get it under control. For everyone. For every child cowering in the shadows right now, powerless and afraid."

A scream clenched in her throat.

"You son of a bitch," she rasped. But she couldn't hate him. He was right. And he had done it, hadn't he? Given power to her voice for the first time ever, there in that awful stinking room, all those years ago. "Go. I've got this."

Marco gave her a final pleading look before walking away briskly.

As Elena reached in anger for the door, her phone began to buzz and ring. Pulling it from her pocket, she noticed the country code on the call.

Germany. Mom or Dad. Who gave them my goddamn number? Probably the President. That dumb Ken-doll-in-chief is always screwing things up.

She declined the call, sending a simple text in lieu of answering: *I'm fine. Busy.*

They had been estranged for so many years that she could hardly remember their faces or voices. The ousting of the Institutional Revolutionary Party and a series of criminal corruption investigations had sent her parents rushing into exile almost two decades ago, returning to the ancestral lands her mother's grandparents had abandoned in the 1930s. Elena had been deep into her university studies at the time and had breathed a sigh of relief—there would now be great physical as well as emotional distance between her and the people who had failed to keep her safe as a child.

Without checking to see if they'd responded to her curt message, Elena stepped back inside the conference room.

"So you're saying they've arisen before?" Silvia Campa was asking Becerra. "Seems tough to believe. There's certainly nothing like that thing in the fossil record, is there, Astrid?"

The biologist shook her head. "No, definitely not. Everything I've seen suggests this—shoo, shookoh—

"Xiuhcoatl," Becerra offered. "I'll say it slower: shoo-KOH-ah-tul."

Elena cleared her throat. "Don't use that term. You'll just confuse the military. For them, the *xiuhcoatl* is the assault rifle we developed for the Army to replace the HK G3."

"Alright, then," Astrid continued. "The *fire wyrm* appears not to be terrestrial in origin."

Esteban Flores took off his glasses but made no move to clean them. "If it came from space, however, it must have been quite some time ago. It emerged from the magma. How long was it there? Why emerge now?"

"And if you're right," Silvia said to Alfonso, "that there are more and they've emerged before, then what stopped them in the past? Like I say, no signs of a 150-meter tall creature have ever been discovered. It dwarfs anything this planet has produced."

Elena waited. Both Marco and the President wanted her to let the archeologist make his case. Fine. The real work had already been done, by her and her team, over five years. While the origin and nature of the hostile were important, she was confident her weapon would suffice to defeat it.

Right now, she decided simply to observe. It made more sense to allow the others to interrogate Becerra, who even now lifted his hands as if to ward off all the questions. "Let me lay out the different pieces of my hypothesis. First of all, the background. Xiuhcoatl was considered to be the physical form of a *Huehueteotl*, an Old God. Not much is known about those most ancient of deities, except that chief among them was Xiuhtecuhtli, the Lord of Fire and Time, father of volcanoes. Huitzilopochtli, the Mexica's God of War, also wielded a fire wyrm as a weapon, the codices tell us. Now, at the end of the First Age, the giant humans and enormous demigods who peopled the earth were destroyed, sources say, many of them encased in stone, a sort of eternal slumber. These huge stones are called...uh..."

Becerra rifled through his backpack till he found an old leather-bound book, some its pages marked with post-its. He flipped around till he found a passage.

"*Quinamehtli. Quinamehtin*'s the plural form. Here's a passage: '*In huehcauh tlacahuiyaqueh mocuepqueh temeh, quinamehtin ipan moquixtihqueh in ihcuac omomiquilih ocelotonatiuh, nahui ocelotl.*' Sorry. I get carried away ... Nahuatl is my family's native language. Translation: 'The bones of the ancient giants became stone, transformed into boulders when the First Sun, Four Jaguar, died.' Now tell me if that doesn't sound like our 'hostile organism,' colleagues."

It was a bit more than Elena could stomach, especially the nonsense about the First Age, which reminded her immediately of his strange rant on her show two years earlier.

"Oh, please. Are you really going to start with the ages and giants again?"

Roberto Menchaca leaned back suddenly, flipping his tie into alignment as realization crossed his face. "Oh, wow. You're *that* Dr. Becerra. What did she call you? 'The Jaime Maussan of Archeology.' You had that crazy hypothesis, uh..."

Astrid nodded, drumming her fingers on the conference table beside her laptop. "He cross-referenced mentions of multiple ages in different mythologies across the world and proposed that the repeated tales of destruction and recreation of the world and its inhabitants meant that sentient hominids had evolved separately at least five times. You know, that's not so at odds with the fossil record, Dr. Baz."

Elena wanted to shake the younger scientist by her scrawny little shoulders. "He claimed that all these beings that purportedly lived in our mythic past—giants, elves, dwarves, trolls—were remnants of those lost sentient species, Astrid. That's *certainly* not consistent with our understanding of human evolution, I'm sure you'll agree."

"Well, to be fair," Becerra responded, flashing that sheepish grin that Elena found so irritating, "I was actually talking about beings from Mesoamerican myth, aluxes and the like, what the Yaqui collectively called *Surem*. Remnants of dead-end evolutionary branches. Of course, though to my face you seemed tolerant of a hypothesis that challenged your worldview, when you edited the episode, you sure did your best to make me look like an idiot. But, hey, no worries. Sales of my book went through the roof as a result, so…yeah. Thanks."

She didn't want to feel defensive, wished she could just shrug off his insinuations without remarking on them, but the archeologist had a knack for getting under her skin.

"I don't *edit* the show, Dr. Becerra. There are producers and others in charge of that sort of thing. But I won't apologize for their choices. You went out on a professional limb, and it snapped beneath the weight of your bullshit."

Silvia shook her head. "Alright, that's enough. I'm playing the age card now and insisting everyone behave. Elena, he's got some questionable hypotheses, but these ideas can help us conceptualize the problem."

Swallowing heavily, Elena nodded and forced herself back into observer mode, allowing the geologist to act the matriarch. Becerra flushed beneath his mahogany skin before giving a thumbs-up.

Silvia continued. "So, I think we can agree on a couple of things. Probable extraterrestrial origin. Fire wyrms and *quinamehtli*? Useful nomenclature. What else?"

Esteban looked up from his tablet. "You called this one shochi…?"

"Xochitonal. That's *show-chee-TOH-nahl*. Spelled with an X. It was the blue-green lizard monster that guarded the entrance to Mictlan, the Aztec Underworld."

"Pretty apt, then. But it's still a stretch to believe that the existence of massive monsters was preserved down the millennia in myths and codices."

"The circumstantial evidence," Becerra responded, "is extensive. For example, take the legend of the three volcanoes. Nahuatl speakers in Morelos have preserved the story for centuries: as in other versions, Popocatepetl and Iztaccihuatl are lovers, but here they are titans of some sort. Then the Nevado de Toluca—another titan—decides it wants Iztaccihuatl as its mate. The rivals begin to throw enormous chunks of ice at each other until Popocatepetl manages to slice the Nevado de Toluca's head clean off, which is why its summit is flat. Makes you wonder whether some deep cultural memory is preserved in these ancient stories."

Elena felt the irresistible urge to retort, but Silvia beat her to it. "Come, now, Dr. Becerra. Clearly, volcanoes are not titanic beings frozen in place by the gods."

"Of course not. But the idea that a similar massive explosion might have in the distant past released a fire wyrm or three on Mexico...not outside the realm of possibility, is it? If I'm not mistaken, 10,500 years ago the Nevado de Toluca exploded with a staggering VEI 6."

In preparation for her now-canceled episode on volcanoes, Elena had studied the major eruptions in Mesoamerica, and she gave a slight nod now. "You're not wrong. However..."

"Oh, I get it. You need some empirical, testable proof that the eruption was connected to the emergence of a fire wyrm."

The smugness that had been glinting in the archeologist's eyes now came fully forward as he smiled at her. Her myoelectric hand clenched with involuntary instinct as her muscles twitched, preparing for whatever ace he clearly held.

"How's this? Nearly two years ago, Ruth Garibay— paleontologist colleague of mine at UNAM—was overseeing a dig near the Nevado de Toluca. At the layer of strata from that eruption, she found something she had trouble believing. Funding ran out, and she couldn't pursue an investigation. In fact, fearing people like Elena here, she kept her discovery under wraps, though she eventually reached out to me, wanting to propose a collaborative project." He shook his head wistfully. "I was getting it ready for submission this morning, actually."

Exasperated and nervous all at once, Elena interrupted. "Cut to the chase, Dr. Becerra."

"You bet. Bring the monitors back up. I need to cast a photo."

Elena picked up the remote and turned on the screens. There was a flicker as Becerra connected to the military intranet, and then an image filled the wall. Surrounded by yellow depth markers and metrics to indicate its size, a massive indentation sprawled in the igneous rock, made before the lava flow had cooled, Elena estimated.

It was a three-toed footprint, twenty-three meters in length.

Identical to those left by—she couldn't help but use the stupid name herself—the fire wyrm.

No wonder the President brought him on board. Sneaky little bastard. He just wanted the satisfaction of showing me up in front of the group.

Silvia sucked in air audibly and said what everyone was clearly thinking.

"Okay, you've got our attention. Wish you had led with this, but we're listening."

Becerra looked at Elena, waiting. Through gritted teeth, she gave him the smallest sliver of what she guessed he wanted.

"Alright. It's obvious that there have been others. I'll grant you that. But what does ancient mythology do for us? How can it possibly help the military defeat..." the name caught in her throat "... Xochitonal?"

"So this is where I'm digging deep, putting researchers across the country into overdrive, gleaning what they can. The traditions go back thousands of years in the archeological record. The Olmecs, for example, worshipped volcanoes."

Silvia tapped her laptop. "Good time to mention that CENAPRED is monitoring all volcanoes across the nation with intense focus. There've been tremors in several places, probably aftershocks. Dr. Becerra ... Alfonso ... doesn't it make sense that an area ringed by volcanoes would evolve religions that revered them?"

"Sure, Silvia. That's clearly one possibility. But consider this: the Olmecs began the tradition of erecting pyramids based on the form—and ritual function, it seems—of volcanoes. And fire wyrm analogues abound in these pyramids. War serpents, feathered snakes, massive lizards of one sort or another. Here's an interesting tidbit from Teotihuacan: among the 75,000 artefacts discovered there recently in a tunnel beneath the Temple of the Plumed Serpent, there were three lozenge-shaped stones, about the length of my forearm, into which the image of a reptilian creature was carved nearly 2,000 years ago."

With a few keystrokes, he sent this image to the screens. Elena had to admit there was a striking similarity in the shape of the stones and the quinamehtli that had floated to the surface of the magma in Popocatepetl's caldera, and the carvings did resemble the fire wyrms to some degree.

Esteban cleared his throat. He had been looking at his tablet intently, and now he gestured at it with a shaky hand. "Odd that you should mention Teotihuacan."

Elena's pulse began to race. "Why?"

"It's all over the news. Here, watch."

The astrophysicist sent the video stream to the monitor. News copters were circling the ruins of Teotihuacan from a safe remove. Their cameras had zoomed unsteadily in on Xochitonal—the fire wyrm was striding its behemoth way up the Avenue of the Dead toward the Pyramid of the Sun. A dozen jet fighters, the US flag flashing like blood on their wings, swept back and forth above it, pounding the titan with missiles, bombs, and cannon fire. A reporter gave shaky voice-over narration as the attack continued.

"You'll note again how the creature—which Army dispatches are now calling a *fire wyrm*—simply shrugs off this intense barrage of firepower as it continues toward the third largest pyramid in the world."

As Xochitonal quickened its lumbering pace, it bent its torso and reached both claws down, scooping up handfuls of large stone blocks from the crumbling walls lining the avenue. With a snarl and twist of its arms, it hurled tons of rock through the sky, missing all but one of the jets, which exploded in a hail of fiery ruin.

"The fire wyrm obviously has a devious intelligence," the reporter opined. "And not even fighter pilots from the USA can protect themselves from its attacks!"

Xochitonal reached the Pyramid of the Sun and ascended its slope like a person might a simple stepladder. Rearing back its head, it stretched forth that slimy, pearlescent inner jaw and began to howl. The image flickered wildly on the screen.

"Our mics are having a hard time ..." the reporter's voice began to cut in and out "... helicopter is shuddering ... perhaps low-frequency ... out of harm's way ... back to you in the studio ..."

Becerra looked over at Elena pointedly. "See what I mean? We have no idea what might happen if you use the ELF cannon. You might awaken more."

"That's pretty unlikely. Even if there are more, they're encased in ... *quinamehtin*, floating in magma. How could they possibly navigate their way out of a volcano *on purpose*?"

The archeologist gave a simple shrug and turned back to the monitor. As the video feed jittered and Teotihuacan grew smaller, Xochitonal crouched and then leapt into the air. The Pyramid of the Sun began to buckle as the fire wyrm hung for the briefest of moments above it. Then the titan's hind legs came smashing down on the ancient temple, hammering it flat and raising a maelstrom of dust and debris.

"Apotheosis," Becerra muttered.

Elena glared at him as if he'd spoken in tongues. "What are you on about now?"

"The name of the place. Teotihuacan. It means 'place where one becomes a god.' I think Xochitonal just assumed its divine mantle."

CHAPTER SIX: ALFONSO

It was a working lunch, of course, with everyone choosing widely different items from the commissary menu. Alfonso was lifting a nopalito taco to his mouth and reviewing an email when he heard Elena make a sound of sardonic surprise.

"Would've never pegged you for a vegetarian."

He glanced up at her in amusement. He had paid her back pretty solidly, though not in front of millions of viewers, so he figured she deserved her weak moment of snark.

"No, this isn't some weak-ass philosophical Buddhist show," he explained pointedly, remembering her refusal to admit to the press that she was an atheist. "My diet's been de-colonized. I eat what my ancestors ate—beans, squash, maize, chia, amaranth, cactus, turkey, iguana, all that good stuff. And you? Some mutton, bread and cheese? Or maybe bratwurst and sauerkraut?"

"Hey, no need to bring race into this. Forget I said anything."

As she walked away and slammed her salad down on the conference table, Alfonso thought of his grandmother's cooking: her plantain memelas with black beans, her yucca tamales, her sweet tlaxcales. Life had moved so much differently there in his hometown of Zongolica, nestled in the mountains of Veracruz. After its initial conquest and conversion under Spanish rule, the insular community had remained cut off from most of the goings-on in Mexico until the mid-twentieth century, when the first highway was carved into the sierra between the city of Orizaba and Zongolica. The isolation had allowed the local dialect of Nahuatl to be preserved alongside Spanish, as well as pre-

Colombian customs and religious beliefs to blend organically with those brought from Europe.

Alfonso's was a working-class family in Zongolica that spoke Nahuatl in their humble home. As a child, Alfonso had arisen early each day to help his father, thrilling to the thick banks of mist that shrouded the valleys above which the snowy peak of Orizaba loomed like a giant on the horizon. He had often pretended he lived among the clouds with the Xocoyoles, mischievous spirit children who wielded wind and rain and lightning with impish delight.

His free time had been spent rambling unsupervised through that green paradise that glistened wet with the spray of waterfalls. Most exciting to him had been to explore the many caves around Zongolica, an experience that had marked him forever, part of the reason he eventually chose to study archeology. The other contributing factor was community tradition, which whispered of lost and arcane knowledge, some of it—the shamans claimed—preserved in a legendary codex known as *The Book of Forbidden Songs.*

Driven by this passion and heritage, Alfonso had become the first in his family to attend college, working two jobs and taking on periodic singing gigs as he did a Bachelor's in archeology and then a Master's in anthropology at the Universidad Veracruzana. After stellar fieldwork that had put his name on the map, he had gone on to pursue a Doctorate in Mesoamerican Studies from UNAM.

Ironically, the very background that—to his own mind, at least—helped make him a consummate conservationist of indigenous culture also lessened his objectivity in the eyes of scientists like Elena who insisted on the dominance of Western empirical research and rejected out-of-hand any native paths to knowledge at odds with those tenets.

The phone near Elena rang.

"Yes?" she answered. "Understood. We'll observe and provide feedback as needed. No, nothing yet. I'll let you know as there are developments on that front. Sure."

She set the handset down on its cradle and brought the monitors back up.

LORDS OF THE EARTH

"Okay, everyone. Xochitonal has finally moved into an unpopulated area on the border between the states of Mexico and Hidalgo. The caravan with the ELF cannon has moved into its apparent path. The Army is preparing to bombard the fire wyrm with subradio frequencies at a level that should disrupt its physical processes, incapacitating or possibly killing it."

On the screen, camera feeds from military drones showed Xochitonal reaching a partially mined-out series of hills a few kilometers from the small town of San Agustín Zapotlán. Military vehicles were deployed all around the area, including two large flatbed trucks that carried the ELF cannon and its power source. A group of technicians swarmed over the cannon as the fire wyrm approached, lowering its head in a gesture that suggested curiosity.

"Now!" hissed Elena, her bionic hand tightening into a fist. "Before it gets too close!"

The Army waited another full minute before switching on the cannon—the indicator lights around the dish went from yellow to green, and the video feed began to shake a little as spillage from the beam sent eddies of sound swirling through the atmosphere.

Though it was impossible to see the sonic wave hitting Xochitonal, there was an audible gasp in the conference room as the titan's forward movement suddenly stopped. Hunching over, it appeared to push against some invisible barrier, baring its teeth in frustration.

"Increase the power, increase the power, come on, damn it." Elena's muttered mantra put everyone even further on edge. One of Xochitonal's arms was wrenched back suddenly, and its tail slammed into the bare rock of the hills, providing greater stability as the fire wyrm strove to advance.

Then, inexplicably, the technicians angled the cannon down, at Xochitonal's legs.

"No," gritted Elena. "What the hell are you doing?"

As the sonic beam pounded its legs, Xochitonal struggled to compensate, but soon its claw-like feet were swept out from under it. As the titan began to fall, its tail flung boulders into the air, arcing toward a cluster of vehicles. Its massive body slammed into the ground with such force that a vast cloud of dust flew up, curtaining the scene for a moment.

When the haze cleared, Alfonso saw that several trucks had been smashed. The flatbed containing the ELF cannon had tilted sideways, sending its beam hammering against the ground. Xochitonal was already regaining its feet, howling with inchoate rage. Several surface-to-air missiles were launched against it from the back of military vehicles, pushing the fire wyrm deeper into the hills, away from the ELF cannon.

"Shit," muttered Silvia. "Everyone get ready for possible tremors. We're sitting on an old lakebed that vibrates with a particular low-frequency pitch. From what Elena's told us, I'm betting her weapon is stirring up some lovely vibrations deep in the bedrock that are going to act like earthquake waves."

Elena punched the table, furious. "These morons don't know what the hell they're doing! Probably put that asshole Felipe in charge instead of Beatriz, inept macho bastards…"

She stomped over to the door, shaking her head.

"Where are you going?" Alfonso asked.

"To chew Marco's ass out, that's where. You people need to hurry up on Plan B just in case the cannon has been damaged."

As the door hissed shut, Esteban looked around at everyone. "Chew the general's ass out? Who the hell does she think she is?"

Roberto laughed. "She's the Bionic Barbie, man. We're all her cosmic puppets."

Silvia sighed. "She's one of Mexico's most gifted minds. And her father was Secretary of Foreign Affairs. Why, do you two have a problem with a strong female leader?"

Astrid quickly jumped in. "Let's not do this war of the sexes thing, okay? Alfonso, is there anything else you can add? Any lore that might help?"

He swallowed deep. "Alright. Clearly, the appearance in Mesoamerica of a fire wyrm or two 10,000 years ago must have left a continued oral tradition. And we see evidence of precisely that lingering cultural memory."

Casting an image to the screens, Alfonso stood.

"This is an Olmec dragon. Note the eyebrows of flame and bifurcated tongue. This god is one of the most depicted of all supernaturals in Olmec architecture and art. Here's another common reptilian, a zoomorphic figure from Xochicalco we call an *iguana dragon*. And here's an Itzam Kab Ayin—monster earth caiman—from Yucatec Maya ruins. Twin reptilian titans are described in the *Popol Vuh*. I could go on and on. Did you know that in the town of Tequila—in the state of Jalisco—legend claims that a dragon is sleeping beneath the community, its head under the cathedral, its tail deep in the dormant volcano?"

Astrid raised a hand to halt him. "I get it, I do. But here's the real question: we've seen the footprint, but how did the hunter-gatherers living in these highlands 10,000 years ago *get rid of the fire wyrm*? They had nowhere near the resources we can marshal, and look at us."

Unable to object, Alfonso nodded with sober chagrin. "Yeah, no idea, sorry. Like I said before, I've got as many people as I can scouring the few codices that remain, searching for a sliver of lore."

Silvia tapped her laptop screen with sudden ferocity. "Okay, my geology team finally has some data for us. They've wrapped up the preliminary analysis of the quinamehtli from which Xochitonal emerged. One discovery is a series of strange tubules in the surface that may have allowed cilia of some sort to move the stone container through the magma. Inside, they've found traces of strange metal-oxide and silicone molecules, along with arsenate carbon."

Astrid's eyes lit up. "A very exotic biochemistry, then? Lends credence to the extraterrestrial origin we posited."

"Yes. Also, dating of material inside the quinamehtli suggests an age of... 4 billion years or more."

Esteban leaned forward. "Ah, okay, then. Leads me to think that Xochitonal and its fellow fire wyrms may have come to the Earth in these 'pods' during the Hadean Eon—the hellish time period from the formation of the planet to about 4 billion years ago. The crust was partly molten, so I can see a bunch of quinamehtin pelting the surface, sinking, and then emerging down the ages, one by one, as geological pressures forced them out of the mantle."

"Could explain a few odd discoveries," Silvia mused, "like the traces of carbon minerals found in 4.1 billion-year-old zircons in Western Australia a few years ago. We're pretty certain they're remains of biotic life, but that was a pretty hostile environment. If the Earth was being seeded, though…"

The astrophysicist nodded. "Another possibility is that the pods were on the hypothetical planet Theia, whose impact with the Earth may have liquefied most of the rock and formed the moon."

"In either case," Astrid interjected, "since the Solar System was in its infancy, I'd say fire wyrms couldn't have evolved here, but must be from some other area of space."

Alfonso half-listened to the exchange as it became more and more technical, scrolling through the emails that dropped into his inbox every minute or so from colleagues across the nation and around the world. Most were tantalizing hints and suggestive images; none provided any real answer to the threat.

The door opened in the midst of the conversation—Elena was back.

"Good news and bad news, everyone," she announced, her tone calmer than before. "On top of everything else, General Navarro tells me that the Gulf Cartel and the Zetas are threatening to take matters into their own hands if the government can't stop these things."

"I'm not surprised," muttered Roberto. "The President has bungled nearly every other crisis in the last four years. It's one of the reasons the cartels have the backing of common folk in so many places."

No one disagreed, though they kept wary silence. Elena glanced pointedly at the cameras in the room, and the chemical engineer flushed red.

"On the bright side, it looks like the ELF cannon wasn't seriously damaged. They should be able to reset within an hour or so for a second attempt, though I'm going to micromanage …"

She was cut off by a sudden tremor that rattled the floor and set the lights to flickering. The scientists all gave little grunts or cries of shock as they hunkered down in their seats. Silvia ducked under the solid mahogany of the table as plaster dust shook itself free from the ceiling. The monitors shut off with a click and hum.

Elena sat down quickly, bracing herself. Alfonso snatched a book before it vibrated its way to the floor.

After about ten seconds, the shaking stopped. Alfonso looked over at Elena, his heart racing like mad.

"I tried to warn you not to use that thing. What if earthquakes are a trigger and draw them to the surface, huh?"

Elena just glared at him, so he stood.

"Well, now that I've had the shit scared out of me, I'm going to the restroom. You guys should get her caught up on what we've discovered."

The guard outside of the conference room pointed him in the right direction. Inside, he leaned his head against the coolness of a mirror before splashing water on his face.

The fear he had been pushing from his mind for hours overwhelmed him at last, and he shuddered. *This could be it. The end of things. The priests of old claimed that at the close of the Fifth Age, the world would be destroyed by earthquakes. What if this is what the prophecies meant?*

Cursing the Spanish conquistadores and Jesuit radicals who had destroyed most of the pre-Colombian codices they'd found, Alfonso relieved his bladder at a urinal, scrubbing afterwards at his hands as if to remove any trace of European blood trapped in his flesh.

By the time he returned to the conference room, he had regained his composure.

But there was bad news. Of course there was. The screens were back up, and buildings were tumbling to rubble in multiple camera feeds from all across the country.

"Looks like they should've listened to you, Alfonso." Silvia gestured weakly at the devastation. "Earthquakes are rocking the states of Tlaxcala, Puebla, Baja California, Jalisco, and Colima. My colleagues at CENAPRED are clamoring that our monitoring equipment is spiking at multiple sites, with tiltmeters indicating that magma is rising in at least two volcanoes at an unprecedented rate."

Esteban yanked off his glasses and wiped them clear for the first time. "Holy shit. There's crazy telemetry coming in from satellites and buoys, everyone. It's the Gulf of Mexico. Bizarre energy surges from its deepest point, the Sigsbee Abyssal Plain. Hard to tell what's going on because a massive hurricane has just sort of…sprung up on top of it, occluding our readings."

Unconcerned at what the others might think, Alfonso pulled his medallion of Tonantzin out from under his shirt, rubbing his thumb across the image of the goddess and closing his eyes in silent supplication.

He thought of his son, of his parents and siblings, of all the people he loved and respected whose lives now hung in the balance.

Don't leave your children to this doom. Help me find an answer, Divine Mother. Help me stop this devastation.

CHAPTER SEVEN: MARCO

"Turn the goddamn alarms off!" Marco shouted above the din. Lights in the command module flickered for another few moments as generators vied with the main power source. SEDENA HQ was built to withstand stronger quakes than these mere tremors, so its systems continued running with minimal hiccoughs.

"Herrera," he called, and a young technician swiveled in his chair. "Check on the VIP bunker. Was it damaged at all?"

"I was just communicating with them, sir. They're fine. Minimal electrical issues that are already being addressed."

Resisting the urge to call his wife again, Marco nodded. "Put the satellite image of that storm up again."

The cloud cover over the Bay of Campeche had nearly doubled in the last two minutes. The general scanned reports from the National Meteorological Service. Experts scrambled to give answers for the sudden appearance of the storm, but it wasn't even hurricane season, and the water shouldn't have been warm enough to allow its formation. Some speculated that the spike in seismic activity might have vented volcanic gas from the depths of the Sigsbee Abyssal Plain.

"General Navarro, the President insists that you brief him in fifteen minutes. Just you, he clarifies."

Marco glanced at Colonel Salazar. "Roger that, Rodolfo. I'll head to the CO office in a minute. Need to check on the scientists first, see what they've come up with. Keep an eye on the volcanoes and make sure evacuation efforts have been accelerated."

The conference room was much more active now than when he had left the team earlier that morning. Everyone was on their phones, consulting animatedly with different teams while they scrolled through multiple devices, checking messages and scouring data points.

Elena was watching the convoy depart from the hills, having righted the ELF cannon and made the necessary and thankfully minimal repairs.

"General," she acknowledged with a brief nod before lifting the phone back to her ear. "Yes. Okay. If you're sure you can cut it off along that route. Be sure to set up at the lowest available elevation. Firing into the ground must be avoided at all costs."

When she hung up, Elena gestured at the others to halt their conversations as well.

Marco cleared his throat. "I've got to meet with the President in fifteen minutes. What can I tell him?"

Dr. Campa looked over at Elena, who motioned approval with her hand.

"Well, General Navarro," the geologist began, "the short version is that the fire wyrm is definitely extraterrestrial. It arrived on this planet a little over 4 billion years ago, when the Earth was still largely molten rock, and has presumably been dormant till now. Its biochemistry is utterly unlike anything we've encountered. At least one other of its kind emerged in Mexico, when the Nevado de Toluca erupted 10,500 years ago. We suspect that somehow either Paleoamericans—whose primary weapons would have been obsidian-tipped spears—or some force of nature stopped that fire wyrm before it could leave much of an environmental impact, since there is no other evidence of its presence beyond a single footprint. Dr. Becerra hopes to discover some orally preserved record of its defeat that may aid us. We also theorize that these creatures are able to navigate through the mantle of the earth in a rudimentary way and that the subradio blast from the ELF cannon may have served as a homing signal, drawing more toward the surface."

An alert began to sound on Dr. Campa's laptop. "Oh, shit," she gasped. "The Colima Volcano. It's erupting."

Pulse racing, Marco punched up the command module on the phone beside Elena. "Give me whatever video feeds we have of the Colima Volcano, now!"

Three of the screens switched to monitoring stations some kilometers distant; the fourth showed satellite imagery.

A massive plume of ash streamed into the sky, rocketing faster and faster as explosion after explosion burst the caldera open. Huge waves of lava came spilling forth, rushing down the slopes at breakneck speed. A final detonation ripped a gargantuan hole in the northeast face of the volcano, and a quinamehtli was flung free, slamming into the pyroclastic flow and sliding like a demonic torpedo toward the flaming tree line below.

Two of the cameras shorted out as the shockwave hit them.

"Get drones out there," Marco rasped into the phone, his voice thick with apprehension. "We need to see what it does, where it heads."

Adjustments made to the satellite feed focused the image on the smoking pod. As the scientists and general watched in silence, its surface cracked open and glittering green talons levered the stone edges apart.

Then a new fire wyrm emerged, steaming and howling, into the ash-darkened hell that was pooling around the northwestern roots of the Transvolcanic Belt. Its chitinous outer skin coruscated deadly green in the lurid light as it stepped into the lava stream and bent forward, burying its talons in that red-orange flow. Then it opened its reptilian outer jaws, pushed forward its pale inner face, and shuddered again and again.

Dr. Campa's computer dinged lightly, drawing her eyes away from the screens. "Um, the volcano observatory at the University of Colima is reporting strange tremors at a frequency similar to the one used by the ELF cannon, traveling in odd patterns through the bedrock."

Elena inhaled sharply.

"What?" Marco asked.

"Shit. I think … I think it's calling the other one."

She grabbed the remote and pulled up a drone video feed of Xochitonal, which had been making its ponderous way toward the

Sierra Madre Oriental. The fire wyrm slowed and then stopped, crouching down to lay its hands flat against the ground.

Dr. Becerra sighed, leaning back in his chair and rubbing his eyes. "Again, I don't mean to say *I told you so*, but I sort of did."

"Look, it isn't my fault the engineer in charge decided to sweep its feet out from under it—he probably watches too much wrestling or something. Now that I'm in charge of the attack, things will be ..."

Becerra had stopped listening to her. Eyes wide, he searched through his backpack till he found another book and creaked it open.

"Alfonso?" Astrid asked. "Got an idea?"

The archeologist began rifling through the pages. Slapping his finger against a page, he read aloud in a foreign tongue. *"Sipakna—are' chirecha'h ri nima'q huyub'."*

"What's that, more Nahuatl?" Marco demanded.

"No, K'iche'. It's a line from the ancient Maya book *Popol Vuh*: 'Sipakna—it guarded the great volcanoes of the world.' Sipakna was the massive reptilian god of earthquakes, jade-green child of Wuqub' Kaqix, a flying demon that fancied itself both sun and moon. Sipakna created volcanoes 'in a single night,' according to the text, and killed four hundred titans—*four hundred* being shorthand for 'uncountable multitude' in many Mesoamerican tales."

"Wait," Esteban said. "I remember this from school. The titans became the Pleiades when they died, right? Then, uh, Sipakna was defeated by the Hero Twins. How? Can that help us?"

The archeologist shook his head. "Not really. The Hero Twins lured Sipakna into a cave at the base of a mountain. Then the mountain settled, trapping it. Over the ages, Sipakna turned to stone. So you see, more of an origin story for our fire wyrms than any useful techniques. We can't exactly drop a mountain on them."

There is something the Americans can drop, however. Marco shuddered at the thought.

Elena smirked. "Fine, Becerra. Xochitonal and Sipakna. We're all willing to accept that Mesoamerican mythology may hold clues to defeating these things, but you've just proven my point—it's pretty freaking unlikely. Until you've got something tangible, the ELF cannon is our best hope."

Dr. Menchaca, the chemical engineer, raised a skeptical eyebrow. "Against both? How much destruction will this new one—Sipakna—cause while you're hopefully killing the first one and then transporting the weapon across the country?"

"Well, I don't hear you offering up a solution, Roberto. How's your team coming with developing a compound that can eat through that armor, huh?"

"How's that fair? We're not even certain of their actual composition, let alone ..."

Before Marco could cut short the nascent argument, the archeologist's phone buzzed, and he bent his head to peer at the screen. "Might have a lead. One of my colleagues has found a reference to the titanic *Cemanahuaquehqueh*—Lords of the Earth—in a sixteenth-century letter by Franciscan priest. He's scanning it to me now. Hopefully, we'll find a clue of some sort so we can track down what was used to stop them."

Glancing at his watch, Marco grunted. "Keep at it, folks. I've got to meet with the President. Can't say he'll be happy at the slow progress."

#

He wasn't. After the general had outlined the findings of his team of experts, the commander-in-chief growled a series of intense expletives.

"And I don't give a shit about where these big bastards come from. I just want them taken out. ASAP. We've now got the Sinaloa Cartel threatening to co-opt us if we can't get our shit together. Multiple countries—most significantly the USA and Russia—are handing down ultimatums. You know what my American counterpart just told me on the phone, Marco? 'Your Mexican monsters can't be allowed to reach the US border. Don't force our hand.' Like we're herding the sons of bitches or something. They want to use nukes, General. Want us to draw the fire wyrms into a deserted area and drop a freaking American A-bomb on them. You know what? I'm inclined to let them. The press and popular opinion has skewered me over the loss of a few dozen journalists and students—imagine what they'll do to me when this is over. No, I need to make some hard choices, fast."

Marco's guts froze as he imagined the fallout—real and sociopolitical—of such a decision. The fire wyrms might die, but Mexico would be plunged into utter chaos.

"Hold on, sir. I assure you that the ELF cannon will be successful. The failure of our first attempt was merely a hiccough. I've met with Dr. Baz and we have agreed that she needs to have operational control on our second bout. No one understands the science behind the weapon better than she does. She is confident that she can make the on-the-fly battlefield adjustments necessary to incapacitate the creatures."

The President leaned toward the telepresence camera.

"That's not enough. I want her ass *in the field*, General Navarro. None of this relaying orders over the phone bullshit. What if there's another tremor or something else cuts SEDENA off from the caravan? She needs to physically be there, do you understand me?"

Swallowing heavily, Marco saluted. "Yes, Mr. President."

"Good. Now go and kill those goddamn monsters, Marco."

#

Telling Elena was going to be tough. He had no desire to put her in harm's way, and he couldn't imagine she would be eager to delve into danger, despite her hard-ass, take-charge attitude. But the President had an undeniable point.

Marco had just passed the command module when a series of explosions rocked SEDENA HQ. A chunk of plaster from the cement ceiling collapsed right in front of him, and the general took a few steps back, staring at the dust, wondering what new development had decided to complicate an already shitty day.

That's when he saw them—a half-dozen men in the blue and white uniforms of the Red Cross, making their way through the clearing haze, the black straps of their gear crisscrossing their chests.

EMS. Pretty fast. Must've been working nearby.

Then one of them saw him and swung a machine gun up.

Instincts honed over years in the Special Forces Corps kicked in, and Marco dove out of the way, rolling to a crouch in a doorway as bullets sprayed down the hall.

It's the goddamn Zetas, he thought, hands balling into fists as they quickened their approach.

"Hang on!" one of them shouted. "That's a high-ranking officer. We need him for access."

Marco listened as a man approached, cautious, rifle firmly against his shoulder. When the Zeta was close enough, the general uncoiled violently from his crouch, slamming his fist into the man's balls, slapping the barrel away with his other hand as his body unbent, then turning sideways and catching the criminal's face with his open palm, yanking him down against the concrete floor with a sickening crack.

Within seconds, he had stripped the invader of his assault rifle and pistol and was opening fire on the other Zetas.

Alarms started to sound; red alert LEDs flickered up and down the hall. As men fell beneath his bullets, fled, or ducked into open rooms, Marco realized he could make out the sound of gunfire behind him. The Zetas had reached the command module.

The general didn't turn to aid his officers and technicians, however. Instead, he sprinted forward, pivoting to exchange fire with a few stragglers as he hurried to the conference room.

In his mind's eye, he saw Elena as a child—waif-thin, nearly dead from blood loss, eyes sunken and haunting against that cadaverous white skin. She reached up her only arm. Her voice was an almost inaudible whisper, hoarse from days of screaming.

Not again. Never again, Elena. I swore it.

A man leapt out at him from a storage room; Marco spun partly out of his way, blocking the hand that brandished a knife and then slamming his fist repeatedly into the back of the Zeta's neck while hyperextending his elbow till it gave a gruesome snap. Then, as the man howled in pain, the general snatched up the blade and drove it up to the hilt in his chin. Death unstrung the criminal's muscles and he dropped like a rag doll to the concrete floor.

Without pausing, Marco continued around the corner to where the guard stationed outside the conference room was fending off several criminals with his handgun. The general sprayed bullets in their direction before ducking into the entrance beside the soldier.

"I had them seal themselves inside, sir," the guard reported. "Told them to barricade the door."

"Good man. Now you're relieved, Private First Class. I've got this. Head down to the command module and clear the rest of these bastards out."

"With all due respect, sir, I should stay behind and protect you."

Navarro leaned forward, letting well-hidden menace slide forward in his face. "Do I look like I need your protection, soldier? Get going."

"Sir!" the private gritted with a wobbly salute before barreling away, gun at the ready.

Marco thumbed open the intercom beside the entrance. "Marco Navarro here. I need you to open the door."

There was movement inside, the scraping of chairs across floors. Then someone scanned a passkey and the lock disengaged.

Marco backed into the room, head swiveling to check for additional Zetas in the hall. Then he turned, closing the door quickly behind him.

Most of the scientists were cowering against the far wall, except for Alfonso Becerra—who had moved the chairs and unlocked the door—and Elena. She was standing by the table, clutching the remote like a weapon, a lost look in her eyes.

The screens behind her showed internal security cams. At a glance, Marco saw his men had nearly put down the attempted coup.

"Who are they?"

Elena's voice was small but angry, with just a hint of panic ready to edge in.

"Probably Zetas, from their weapons and tactics. Cartel of the North or whatever they call themselves now. They've been threatening for the last couple of hours to wrest control of the country's defense from the military. I'm guessing the Second Emergence pushed them over the edge. Very foolish, trying to shoot their way into SEDENA HQ."

With nervous twitters and sighs of relief, the other scientists grabbed chairs and dropped heavily into them, muttering about the insanity of it all. Marco walked over to Elena, gave a wry half-grin, and hit the extension for the command module on the phone.

"Colonel Salazar, tell me you've retained control."

Rodolfo's voice was strained but clear. "Yes, sir. We only suffered a few casualties. Mopping up the rest of the cartel henchmen now. Are you okay, General?"

"Yes. I'm with the advisers, ensuring their safety. Let me know when the coast is clear."

Elena touched his left hand tentatively as he closed the connection. His knuckles were bruised and specked with crimson.

"Blood. You had to fight."

Marco turned his eyes on her, struggling against the urge to crush her to him as if she were his own daughter. The heft of the gun in his right fist felt natural, inevitable. A quarter century had sloughed off him in ten minutes of combat. His mind burned deadly bright with single purpose.

"Yes. And I'll keep fighting, Elena. We both will. Since we're not safe even here, it's time we face our real enemy out there in the field."

As the others gasped or muttered invectives, she tensed up, squinting at him as if trying to discern a hidden truth in his features.

"You'll keep your promise, won't you?" she muttered, though everyone could hear.

Marco bit the inside of his mouth, forcing his emotions into check.

"You know I will. Never again, El. Never."

The tension in her form eased away and, to everyone's amazement, she smiled.

"Okay, then. Let's go slay the dragons."

CHAPTER EIGHT: CHARLOTTE

August 13, 1938—

Last night, James came home so terribly exhausted and putout after a grueling day of work that I found I just couldn't broach the subject with him. I warmed up his dinner, and after two fingers of gin, he dropped like a stone into the depths of sleep.

I had a harder time getting any shut-eye, tossing and turning for hours before finding myself in formless dreams in which squirming tentacles lashed out at me from curtains of dark, starlit spray.

I awoke before dawn, loaded tackle and supplies into the utility coupe, and headed down to Port Isabel. Yesterday's fervor had begun to fade, and as I pulled up to the marina, I began to doubt my earlier resolve. Did I really want to ply the Gulf waves, looking for a monster? The idea seemed mad in the pink-tinged light of dawn.

Phelps wasn't on the yacht, but I prepared my gear and carried out an inspection of key systems. Other would-be competitors were already stirring on the boats around me.

Before long, Sally Crowe, secretary for the rodeo, came up alongside the *Siren Spray* and called to me.

"Morning, Sally," I replied, emerging from the cabin.

"I'm just verifying who's still in, Charlotte. Yesterday several fishermen decided to withdraw their names."

"Oh, I wouldn't dream of not competing."

"That's what I figured. Folks keep talking about how you want to catch the 'monster.' I think you'll be disappointed, though."

"How's that?"

"Really, Charlotte? A monster? I hardly think so. It's more likely a basking shark. That's one of the larger members of the shark family, you know."

Her little lecture was annoying. "I know what a basking shark is, Sally. How in the world did you reach this conclusion of yours?"

"Well, it's simple, silly. I just picked up a dictionary and started flipping through, thinking about the descriptions some people have given. I stopped at every picture of a fish—and there it was on page 180. Basking shark."

"Ah, that was clever," I said in a sardonic tone that I knew she'd not notice. It was just like her to take the theories of experts and pretend that she had thought them up on her own. "But no matter what the thing turns out to be, yes, I'd like to be the one who catches it. I'm not bowing out. Keep me in the open competition, okay?"

Sally nodded cheerfully and ambled off to interrogate others. As Phelps still hadn't returned from whatever errand had drawn him from the yacht, I decided to head over to the wharf where the Mexican fishing boats make their berth. Any new information might give me an edge in the hunt that seemed more and more likely.

After asking around in broken Spanish and getting garbled repetitions of tales I had already heard, I was startled by the clanging of a bell and the shouts of anxious sailors. Turning my head, I saw a good-sized seiner come careening into port, smacking up against pylons before men and boys dropped from its decks in a panic.

Stopping one sunbaked youth, I asked in my halting, gringa way, "¿Qué pasa?"

"Un monstruo," the teen replied breathlessly. "We see a monster. Media unos cuarenta metros de largo. Forty!" He stretched his arms wide to emphasize the gargantuan size.

I was a little dubious. "What's your name? Tu nombre."

"Carlos. Carlos Serrano."

"Okay, Carlos. I need to talk to one of the men. Can you take me to one?"

"Yes. My tío ... uncle. Come, señora."

Trotting ahead of me, the youth called out to an older man who was twisting a line around a mooring. Behind him on the hull was the seiner's name: the *Doña Angélica*.

"What language did you just use?" I asked as we approached. "Not Spanish, was it?"

"No, señora. Huasteca. Language of our village. Al sur de Tamaulipas. Far south."

The sailor straightened as he saw me. Carlos gave a quick, animated explanation.

"Do you speak English?" I asked.

"A little."

"Can you tell me what happened?"

He flexed his fingers nervously, his thick knuckles popping. "We are at sea for four days, net in the water. Then when the sun comes on day five, a very big thing passes under the boat. Rips net off. Almost sinks the boat. Takes our catch ... a lo profundo."

Swallowing heavily, I nodded. "To the deep. Did you see it? Was it a shark?"

He shook his head and spat to one side. "No shark. Never seen nothing like. Not normal."

Thanking Carlos and his uncle, I walked away, definitely intrigued. Back at the marina, I rounded up several of the women still committed to the rodeo—Margaret Duemler, Janice Marchman, Jody Goolsby, Lucy Landers, Evelyn Sullivan, and Haley Oler.

"Forty feet long," I told the women after recounting that morning's events. "That's what the boy said. Can you imagine catching something as massive? Now *that* would be a feat for the record books. Who's in?"

Though Janice and Evelyn declined the offer, the rest agreed to join me. The idea is for us to meet tomorrow on the *Siren Spray* and have Phelps take us out after the monster. I've arranged for the delivery of extra harpoons, 500 feet of rope, and a dozen tightly plugged barrels. My plan is to spear the creature and keep it from sounding so that we can haul it back to the Laguna Madre.

The problem, sad to say, is James. When I came home late this afternoon, he was waiting for me, the *Herald* folded neatly beside him on the sofa.

I immediately realized my mistake. Caleb had used my little diatribe in a damn article.

"When were you planning to tell me of this 'monster hunt' of yours?"

I knelt before him, taking his hands in mine. "James, love, don't be angry with me. You were exhausted last night. I simply didn't want to agitate you."

"Oh, I'm agitated, alright, Charlie." It's his nickname for me. "And I want you to forget this craziness. I spoil you rotten in other ways, let you run around like a man with your peculiar passions, but I'll be damned if I'm going to sit here while you endanger your life in pursuit of some massive predator that no one can properly identify."

Despite my love for him, I couldn't help but bristle at this masculine arrogance.

"And I'll be damned," I said, lifting my hands from his, "if I'm going to allow you to dictate the terms of my life to me. I told you when you proposed to me—I'm no man's possession."

His expression went cold. "The yacht is mine, even if you're not. You'll not take *Siren Spray* out on the Gulf. I forbid it."

I exploded at him. We hurled ugly sentiments back and forth. The argument lasted for the better part of an hour, concluding with my banishing James to the guest bedroom before locking myself in for the night.

I still feel tremors of righteous ire. Look at my letters, twisting as if they flowed from palsied fingers. A few days at sea will calm me and give him time to reflect. For now, I'll try to sleep.

August 14, 1938—

That son of a bitch.

This morning I awoke later than I had planned after a long and restless night full of bizarre nightmares. James was already gone. Readying myself as quickly as feasible, I drove down to the marina to find *Siren Spray* gone and my co-adventurers scattered. Only the barrels, harpoons, and rope sat useless on the quay, mocking me.

It was Sally who came round at last, a damnable smirk on her face that I was tempted to erase with my fist. She was dolled up in her Sunday best.

"Hello, dear." She looked me up and down, eyes lingering on my sport pants and bush shirt with pointed disapproval. "On my way to church, but I wanted to verify this in person. They tell me your husband stopped by early. I gather he asked Captain Phelps to take his yacht to Galveston for servicing. Then he had the operator ring me up and explained that you wouldn't be competing this year."

Resisting my desire to jump over the railing, rip the Bible from her hands, and beat her around the head and shoulders with it, I gritted my teeth and shook my head.

"No, Sally. I'm not withdrawing. Keep me on the registry."

"How will you compete without a boat?"

"Let me worry about that. I'll give you the details tomorrow."

With a sarcastic shrug, she left to play sweet innocent Christian at the Episcopalian church. For a while, I just leaned against one of the barrels, my emotions swirling impotently. Then I wandered the nearly lifeless docks for a while, fuming at James and considering my next move.

Finally, realizing I needed more information, I decided to drive to the Coast Guard's Padre Island station to speak with Captain Pablo Valent.

Guess who was already waiting to meet with the commander? Caleb from the *Herald*.

"Hey, thanks for ruining two days of my life, pal," I grunted at him.

"What are you talking about? The article? You're the one who made the statements, Mrs. Sewell. You never said they were off the record."

I sighed and waved away his indignation. "Sorry. Just ignore me. I have a tendency to open my big mouth and complicate my own life."

A petty officer soon called for the reporter, and he invited me to join him since his interview would cover a lot of the same ground as my own questions.

Valent was very upfront about the situation and polite to boot.

"Several additional sightings in the last twenty-four hours have convinced me that something is definitely lurking perhaps a hundred miles off shore. You may have heard that Mr. Burnell is taking a group of men out Tuesday morning to capture the mysterious creature—Mayor Hunt will be on board, along with Dr. Hockaday and other pillars of the community. So we plan to keep a protective eye on the sea monster expedition. I don't imagine that the party will run into trouble, but it is in line with the Coast Guard's duty that we be ready to proffer aid should it be needed. Our boats will be within reach from the time the monster is sighted until it is lost or dragged back to port."

After the meeting, I went home, ready to confront my husband and take him to task for sending Phelps away. But he was gone, so I simply stewed in my juices all afternoon. And I mean that literally, as I must've downed half a bottle of gin before succumbing to its effects. Waking up a while ago in the dark, I found James had draped a blanket over me where I lay on the sofa. He is softly snoring in our bed.

My head is pounding. I'm going to fix myself something to eat and get some more sleep.

Tomorrow, I take action. Burnell and his cronies aren't going to edge me out of this adventure. I'm going to catch the goddamn monster myself.

I've got a plan.

August 15, 1938—

No turning back now.

Up before dawn. Headed for the wharf to look for the *Doña Angélica*. Carlos and his uncle were already moving around the deck, busy with different tasks. The kid was thrilled to see me; his uncle stared at me warily. I requested to speak with their captain.

Eugenio Maldonado is his name, a crusty, sea-weathered fellow of the sort one might root for in a high-seas talkie. His English is impeccable.

"I want to charter your boat, Captain Maldonado," I told him. "Immediately."

His laugh was soft and honest. "Why would you want to hire a seiner, ma'am? You're with the rodeo, no? You don't need a vessel this size to catch marlin."

"It's not marlin I want to catch. I'm after the monster. It may take days to track down. It will certainly take a full crew to harpoon the thing and drag it back to port."

He blanched like I'd never seen such a gruff man do in my life. "First of all, this boat is not mine to hire out. I'm its captain. Angélica Duarte de Palomo owns it. She lives in Matamoros and will be difficult to reach on such short notice. Secondly, you haven't seen the creature. Neither have I. But several of my crew have, and some abandoned fishing altogether because of it. Getting more men and supplies to attempt such a feat? I fear that—"

"I'll pay you a thousand dollars," I interrupted. "For one week, at the most. This operation doesn't make that in two months, I'd wager."

The sum made his eyes light up. He pays his men less than a dollar a day, I had calculated. Rather than sit in port, bleeding profit, I was betting on his wanting to make some off-the-books cash.

"Two thousand," he countered. I was ready for this haggling. It's the Mexican way.

"Twelve hundred."

"Eighteen."

I sighed dramatically. "Fifteen hundred. That's as high as I can go. But I'll supply the harpoons, rope, and barrels. Do we have a deal?"

Easing back into his chair, he drummed his fingers on the hardwood desk.

"Okay. I assume you want to leave before the others."

I nodded. "In the middle of the night, if possible. Can you get your crew and provisions together by this evening?"

"Leave that to me, Mrs. Sewell. You just bring me the money. Everything will be ready."

And so the afternoon found me at the bank, face-to-face with Marvin Stills, one of its officers.

"Does your husband know you're withdrawing this sum?"

I raised an eyebrow at him. "The account is in my name. The funds are mine and have been since before my marriage. What difference can it make to you whether he knows or not?"

I probably should have been more politic about the transaction, but I am frankly fed up with men and their incessant bullshit. In the end, what could Stills legally do? He had no choice but to honor my wishes. Though the arrogant slant of the smug bastard's head made me suspect he might make a few phone calls after I left, I couldn't let that cow me.

James didn't seem the wiser, however, when he came home. I acted as if nothing were amiss. When he abashedly apologized to me—while nonetheless reiterating his desire to keep me safe from my own self-destructive tendencies—I just smiled and said I understood.

It's a little past midnight. He's fallen asleep. The money sits in the steel box inside the utility coupe's trunk, along with my tackle.

I'll take this journal with me as a sort of log.

Time to ply the waves.

CHAPTER NINE: ELENA

Elena had spent more than two decades inuring herself to the sound of gunfire, to the swirling black of despair and impotence. Part of becoming a scientific adviser to the military had been this need to never feel helpless again, to never cower in pain and fear.

When the attack had begun, however, her mind had in an instant translated her to the past, to a filthy room in a squalid shack on the outskirts of Mexico City. Muffled shots—singly and in stuttering sprays—had come from beyond.

"Keep your mouth shut, brat," the Hyena had snarled at her, but by then her preschool voice was ragged and ruined. She couldn't have cried out if she had wanted to.

Suddenly, the door had burst in, and a black-clad form had disarmed her captor with a few quick, vicious moves.

Then Marco had swept her up in his arms.

"Shh…" he had whispered, squeezing her tight against his body armor. "You're okay, Elena. I'm here. No one's going to hurt you ever again."

"You promise?"

"I swear it, sweetie."

But the Hyena had stirred there on the ground. Elena—understanding as if by instinct what would happen—had whispered a command into her rescuer's ear.

Amazingly, he had obeyed.

Now Marco's presence in the conference room—the revered general stripped away, exposing the taut and merciless soldier at his core—brought that final moment to her mind, the power and relief that she felt in wielding another human being as a weapon.

As long as she kept him bound by that oath, she could shape events at this moment of innervating darkness. Armed with his loyalty, she might be able to save her country as he once had saved her.

So, despite the danger, she would go into the field with him and face the monsters, both the one that had haunted her dreams for decades and the new ones that had arisen today from the bowels of the earth.

Esteban was the first of the others to speak.

"Yeah, I'm not sure what's up with you two, but I'm not going to go slay any dragons, guys. I can provide my expertise in perhaps understanding the organisms' extraterrestrial origins, but I'm no soldier."

Marco nodded. "I'm sorry: let me clarify what I mean. The President has insisted that Elena go into the field to supervise and troubleshoot the use of the ELF cannon. Given its present speed, Xochitonal will soon move out of the First Military Region. As a result, I will be leaving my command staff in charge of controlling civil unrest so that I can accompany Elena, providing protection and coordinating with SEDENA the command of forces from my region. No one else is required to go."

Silvia shook her head. "Maybe not, but I want to."

"Yes," Astrid said. "Me, too. I have a feeling that you'll be needing my real-time expertise if the cannon incapacitates or kills the fire wyrm. There's a mobile lab in the caravan, isn't there?"

"Yes, Dr. Estrada. It will be completely at the team's disposal."

Roberto sighed. "Then I guess you can count on me as well. Hopefully the sort of analyses Astrid is hinting at will help me lock down a compound we can use on Sipakna."

Elena glanced over at Alfonso, who was staring at his computer screen and jotting down notes. *Ignoring us. Not surprised.*

The telepresence screen blinked to life. Colonel Salazar stood in the midst of the command module. Behind him, living Zetas were being led away while dead ones were dragged off unceremoniously.

"General Navarro," he said, "we've completely secured HQ, arresting two soldiers on duty at the gate who let the Zetas in."

"Good work. What's the status on the storm and the hostiles?"

"The hurricane is still spinning, stationary. Xochitonal has changed course and is now heading in the direction of Santiago de Querétaro. Our caravan has been rerouted to intercept. The other organism—Sipakna?—is reaching the outskirts of Guadalajara. US-Canadian forces are providing aerial support to our troops there."

Elena's eyes burned as she thought of how many lives might be lost in that city today.

"Colonel," Marco said, "I need you to prep a tactical transport plane, one of the C-295s. Get me a COIFE squad. I'll be taking most of our team to rendezvous with the caravan. You'll oversee efforts to stem civil unrest and to provide emergency services."

Though his brow wrinkled a bit with probable doubt, the officer saluted his general.

"Yes, sir."

As the connection went dark, Alfonso slammed his laptop shut.

"I can't go, General. At least, not right away. I've got a seriously important lead."

A little dubious, Elena crossed her arms. "Well? What is it?"

"I finally received the scan of that letter I mentioned. It was written in Nahuatl on May 7, 1554 by Franciscan friar Bernadino de Sahagún to Juan Badiano, an indigenous professor at the Colegio de Santa Cruz de Tlatelolco. In it, the friar explains why he is excluding certain songs from a manuscript he is compiling—this is the codex that we now call *Cantares Mexicanos*. Lots of excuses—mainly that they're songs of praise for bloodthirsty native 'demons,' as he calls Aztec gods. But he specifically mentions the Lords of the Earth: 'titanic antediluvian devils which long to return to earth. Among the hymns are Satanic spells to appease their vile appetites and keep them at bay.' It seems that Badiano wanted access to these expurgated songs, and Sahagún reluctantly agreed to let him take a look at them."

Elena glanced at the rest of the team to see their reaction before responding with caution.

"Okay, so let me guess: you think that one of these spells might be of use. Do you know where they are?"

Alfonso shook his head. "No, that's the tricky part. This is the first written reference I've ever found to their existence. However, many Nahuatl-speaking communities have a long-standing tradition concerning a *Book of Forbidden Songs*. Some of the songs have been passed down orally for hundreds of years."

Astrid snapped her fingers in understanding. "You come from Zongolica, don't you? And you said your native language is Nahuatl. So your family has kept the old traditions alive, right?"

"Yes. That's why I can't go with you right now. I need to get to my hometown as soon as possible. There's a shaman I can talk to, the man who used to sing those old songs to us when I was a kid. If there's an answer to the fire wyrms in the expurgated lore, he may know it."

Marco sighed. "Well, I wish you luck, Dr. Becerra. I just don't think we have the time. The problem will be resolved in the next couple of hours, one way or another. I doubt your journey into the mountains of Veracruz—even if successful—will bring us an answer quickly enough."

"I get that," Alfonso said, sliding his laptop into his backpack and wrapping up the power cord. "That's why I need you to put me on the fastest plane you have so I can hunt this man up and get back to you in the field before it's too late."

Elena saw the twitch in Marco's cheek, a tell-tale sign of suppressed irritation. "Out of the question, Dr. Becerra. That thing has already decimated our nation's small Air Force. I'm not pulling a jet from the fight just to send you on whatever wild goose chase you've conjured up out of thin air."

Alfonso stiffened, and Elena realized with a start what it was about him that stirred up so much rancor in her—he reminded her of her father, self-righteous in his arrogant piety, always ready to sacrifice logic and reason in the name of his faith.

"I don't think you really have the luxury of dismissing a possible solution," the archeologist muttered, "in such a cavalier way."

"And I'm afraid my patience with your theories has worn thin. The answer's no. It's time for action, not aimless research."

Nodding, Alfonso began to make his way around the far side of the table, passing behind the other four scientists. "It's too bad you feel that way. I didn't want to go over your head, General Navarro, but you're not thinking clearly. Maybe the Zeta attack kicked you so far into combat mode that you can't see the bigger picture right now."

The archeologist walked over to the telepresence control panel on the wall.

"What're you doing, Becerra?" Marco snapped.

"Calling the President. Let's see what he says."

Marco lifted his pistol, aiming it at Becerra.

"Step away from that panel, now."

"No. I don't think you'll actually shoot me. Be really hard to explain that one to your commander-in-chief, wouldn't it, especially as he was the one who put me on this team."

Turning his back on the general, Alfonso opened up a channel to the presidential bunker.

Elena watched Marco's hand tremble for a moment, the knuckles of his index finger whitening as conflicting stresses jerked at his muscles. Then he lowered the pistol, muttering a curse.

The President and the Secretary of National Defense peered at them from the screen.

"Ah, Dr. Baz. Are you ready to supervise the ELF cannon on-site?"

Alfonso spoke faster than she could muster a reply. "She sure is, Mr. President. But this is about another attack vector. I've tracked down a possible response to the fire wyrms, but I need immediate and rapid transport to Zongolica in Veracruz to retrieve the information in person from a source who can't be reached by other means. General Navarro wanted to get, uh, operational clearance from you, however."

That move surprised Elena. Rather than burn Marco for obstructing his research, Becerra had given him a way to save face.

"Well, of course, General! Make it happen. Whatever the team needs, as I've told you before."

Marco hesitated a moment. "Yes, sir. I will be going into the field with the rest of the team—except for Dr. Flores. We need real-time, physical access to the hostile organism when the ELF cannon incapacitates it."

The President nodded. "Good thinking. We'll let the commander of Military Region XII know that you'll be joining the caravan. Keep me updated every fifteen minutes."

The monitor went dead as the connection was closed. Marco stared at the archeologist for a full minute with cold eyes before addressing him.

"You'd better make this worth it, goddamn you."

Punching up the command module on the phone, the general contacted Colonel Salazar.

"Rodolfo, do me a favor and have them prep that old Harrier Matador we got from Spain. We have to transport Alfonso Becerra to Zongolica, Veracruz. And send an armed guard to escort him to the airfield immediately. I want him gone before we board our plane."

Becerra walked back to his chair, slung the backpack over his shoulder.

"Thanks, General. I know you're pissed now, but I'll meet you guys in the field very soon with what I'm sure will be actionable intelligence."

Marco made response, but the set of his jaw said everything.

#

Twenty minutes later, Elena and Marco—along with Silvia Campa, Astrid Estrada, Roberto Menchaca, and six elite members of the Special Forces Corps or COIFEs—were hurtling through the skies of Mexico aboard a C-295 tactical military transport at some 300 mph. The caravan had set up on the border between the states of Hidalgo and Querétaro, right in the projected path of Xochitonal.

Sipakna was, from all appearances, headed for a rendezvous with the other fire wyrm. Elena stared at her tablet, horrified at the scenes of destruction that were being broadcast from Guadalajara. The green titan wreaked even more havoc than Xochitonal, ripping through the Omnilife Stadium, laying waste to the university, felling the glittering towers of Aura Lofts and the Riu Hotel, and viciously kicking the cathedral to ruins.

Social media was overwhelmed by video clips of the devastation, death, and gore left in Sipakna's wake as it made its way northeast. But Elena, shuddering at those tragic snippets of horror, found herself drawn to the larger conversation taking place across the Internet.

It had only been a little over seven hours since the First Emergence, but the world entire was aflame with fear. Riots had broken out in major cities in most nations. People were fleeing areas near volcanoes, panicked at the thought that more fire wyrms might drag themselves from their hellish rest at any moment. There were horrible lines at gas stations and lootings at grocery stores as fearful folk prepared for the worst.

Many religious leaders had announced the arrival of the end times, a purging of the world before the return of one god or another. Elena scowled at these declarations, but found the cries of the Left in her country equally concerning—*the raped earth of Mexico is taking its revenge on a corrupt, capitalist system*, they proclaimed. Then there were the conspiracy theorists who claimed that the President of Mexico had hired a Hollywood production company to stage the whole thing with CGI in order to justify an invasion by the United States.

"Pretty disheartening, isn't it?" Silvia remarked, raising her voice to be heard above the roar of the engines. The military transport was bare of all amenities that might weight it down, including soundproofing of its hull.

"Yeah," Elena told the older scientist, "though I get it. No one trusts the government to solve this crisis. The natural human instinct is to freak the hell out."

"You were alive for the '85 earthquake, right?"

"I was four. But we were on a state visit to Switzerland—my father was, I mean—so we didn't have to live through it."

Of course, two years later, Elena had lived through something even more terrorizing and traumatic. She blinked away the memory, focused on the iron gray of Silvia's bobbed hair.

"I had just started teaching at UNAM," the geologist mused. "I was scrawling something on the chalkboard, and then it was suddenly like the world had been tilted and someone was trying to shake us off. Horrible, horrible day. But we moved past the tragedy, learned to respect the precarious earth beneath our feet, and rebuilt smarter. It's hard for people to see it now, but we will eventually be on the other side of this event. We'll come together and adjust our lives to the new knowledge. It's what we do, human beings."

Elena hoped she was right. It was slow and agonizing, this gradual move away from primitive superstition toward the logical empiricism needed to survive an indifferent cosmos. Sometimes she doubted humanity's chances.

#

The flight only lasted twenty minutes. The C-295 made a rough landing on an improvised airstrip in the Bondojito Ecological Preserve, scant miles from the border between Hidalgo and Querétaro. A pair of jeeps delivered them to the staging area, where the ELF cannon was already being prepped.

"Alright, soldiers," Marco instructed the COIFE team, "I'm going to go meet with Colonel Ortiz. Protect Dr. Baz at all costs. Allow her to do her work, but if you judge her to be in mortal danger, evacuate her at once."

Turning to Elena, he lowered his voice. "I'll be back as soon as I can, okay?"

"Yes, of course. I've got this, Marco."

"Doctors," the general called to Silvia, Astrid, and Roberto, "if you come with me, I'll show you to the mobile lab."

"If it's okay with Elena, I'd like to stay and help her," Silvia replied.

"Of course it's okay. Thanks."

Elena, with the COIFEs and Silvia in tow, made her way to the control terminal a few dozen meters back from the cannon itself. Beatriz Altamira—black eyes flashing beneath unruly curls—was supervising last-minute systems checks.

"Elena!" she called, delighted in her somber sort of way. "So glad you decided to come out and oversee this in person. Also, ahem, thanks for getting Felipe Salinas pulled from the caravan. That stupid son of a bitch, I swear."

Elena found herself laughing despite the grimness of the moment. "You bet. I just hope they court martial his ass. Hundreds more have died after his flub than might have if you'd been calling the shots, Be. Here, let me introduce you. This is Silvia Campa, geologist at UNAM, works with CENAPRED. Silvia, meet Beatriz Altamira, the Army's best computer engineer."

The women smiled and shook hands.

"So, Be, what's Xochitonal's ETA?"

"Ten minutes. What do you need?"

"I've written a script to automate a sequence I've crafted, quick shifts among ultra- and infrasonic-frequencies, using the wyrms' recent 'communication' as a baseline."

Beatriz nodded. "Bad-ass. We can upload it straight into the terminal. Have a drive, or should we tooth it over from your device?"

The two of them quickly imbedded the script in the firing program. Elena's palms tingled with nervous expectation. While Becerra had been drawing others into his little fantasy world, she had been developing this hack of her own weapon. Now it was time to show everyone the power of science, its ability to take the impotent rumblings of sound, and forge a monster-killing weapon with them.

Marco came by as she and Beatriz were working. Thankfully, no sooner had he gotten a hasty status update from them than he was called away to another meeting. Elena didn't need the distraction right now, with just minutes left. Racing against the clock, the team ran simulations to ensure that the new sequence would work.

The crew went down to the wire. When Elena nodded her approval at last, she felt tremors beneath her feet.

"It's coming," Silvia muttered, kneeling and laying her open palm against the dirt. "Seven hundred metric tons, our best guess. A good-sized hill, walking the earth."

As crews scrambled to prepare various batteries of weapons, Elena stood at the terminal, flanked by the other two women, and watched Xochitonal loom into view.

In the clear afternoon light, the fire wyrm's alien nature revealed itself fully, its asymmetrical scales coruscating impossible shades of blue, its eyes twin suns, that prehensile tail searching the ground behind and beside it, snatching up certain living things and somehow devouring them.

The ELF cannon had cycled to readiness, and its eager hum was music to Elena's ears, the murky melodies of untrammeled power. Those tones were joined by quiet chimes from the terminal as the fire wyrm crossed into the range of the weapon.

Elena waited a few seconds more, two strides of those towering legs, gripping the edges of the terminal to steady herself as the earth arced up against her feet as if in pain.

Then she slapped her fingers against the keys, and the ELF cannon shot its high-powered waves up at the titan, frequencies morphing in howling glissandi that halted Xochitonal and set it to twisting in obvious pain.

"Hell, yeah!" screamed Beatriz. "You've got him, El!"

Cranking the power with a horrible smile, Elena adjusted the cannon's angle and orientation as the fire wyrm stumbled backward. All across its torso, chinks opened in its armor, exposing glimpses of slimy white flesh. The concerted firepower of the caravan was instantly concentrated on these gaps—machine guns, mortars, RPGs and small missiles. Xochitonal attempted to turn away from the barrage, but Elena's sequence sped up its shifts till the creature began slapping at itself in slow, twitching arcs of its mighty limbs.

"Come on," Elena gritted as she angled the cannon right at the fire wyrm's head. "Fall, you great green bastard!"

For the briefest of moments, Xochitonal's blazing eyes turned upon her heavily, their inner fire crackling with unfathomable spite.

Then the titan collapsed, its bulk describing a ponderous arc through the smoky traceries of weapons fire. Elena shut off the cannon and shouted at her crew:

"Brace yourselves!"

Beatriz and Silvia both grabbed a hold of the steel frame of the terminal mounting beside her. Around them soldiers dropped flat to the ground, away from the vehicles.

Xochitonal hit the earth, sending many of them flapping into the air like rag dolls. Elena was yanked from her feet and twisted up in Beatriz's flailing limbs, the two of them dropping painfully from the low control platform. Jeeps and transports bounced as well, the two closest to the wyrm flipping onto their sides.

Extricating herself from the engineer, Elena struggled to stand. A firm grip took her arms and helped her. It was Marco.

"My God, El. You really did it. Just like you said. You knocked the shit out of that thing."

Elena surveyed her prey, its enormous form curving before them like some shattered knoll. Bits of chitin had been blasted away and now littered the rocky soil. Teams of technicians, guarded by soldiers, were easing their way toward the quiescent wyrm. No sign of life came from it.

But as the first man reached out an instrument to touch that alien hide, Xochitonal roared back to life, lifting its head and vomiting steaming green bile all over a half-dozen specialists, melting them into immediate sludge. Lumbering up to all fours, it began lashing its tail around, flipping vehicles and uprooting boulders as it rumbled subsonic agony into the bedrock.

"Move, Elena!" screamed Silvia, who had finally recovered and was now descending from the platform.

Elena quailed in terror. She couldn't find the strength to budge, even as Marco yanked at her arm. The fire wyrm whipped its head around and caught sight of her at last, snarling with inchoate intent.

That prehensile, snapping tail whipped out, reaching for her.

In a single quick move, Marco spun her to the ground and shoved Silvia into its path.

Elena found her voice at last.

"No! Silvia!"

But those long, emerald claws sliced the geologist in half. Silvia's eyes were lucid enough to watch her entrails spill blackly upon the dirt as a chittering maw at the end of the tail consumed her lower body.

Elena thankfully saw no more. Marco's screamed orders brought the Special Forces Corps members scrambling over, and they whisked her to relative safety.

The air reverberated with the thundering steps of the fire wyrm as it stood and resumed its devastating trek, pausing only to seize the C-295 and hurl it with ungodly force against the caravan, destroying half of the vehicles in a ball of conflagration.

Elena didn't bother to ask whether the cannon had been damaged.

Silvia's eyes were all she could think of, wide with shock and despair.

CHAPTER TEN: ALFONSO

Alfonso understood the need for a jet capable of vertical take-off and landing—Zongolica was nestled in the mountains and didn't even have a helicopter pad, much less a landing strip—but the two-seater was more cramped and noisier than he could imagine.

Its speed and the odd pilot's unexpected gyrations made him queasy as hell.

"Don't you throw up, Doc," Serio Tinoco warned in his ear. "No barf bags on board. Didn't have time to do more than fuel up and fly."

"I'm good. Don't want vomit in this mask, anyway."

Alfonso distracted himself by reviewing documents he'd saved to his phone, trying to better piece together the pre-historic event that must have given rise to all the later myths across Mexico about reptilian titans. It was a task that required years of research and coordination, but all Alfonso had was a few hours. Even with the aid of hundreds of experts, it was going to be ballpark at best.

Soon the cloud cover broke below, revealing his hometown, wreathed in mist, encircled by rivers and peaks. The sight pulled at his heart like little else could. There was hardly any traffic on the streets, which was unusual. He searched for his family's neighborhood, wishing he could visit them while he was there.

I'll make a point of it when this is all over. Tell the folks I love them. Life is short and dangerous. The emergence of the Lords of the Earth underscores that inescapable fact.

The municipal police had already cordoned off a patch of land at the edge of town at SEDENA's request. Tinoco slowed, spiraled around the edges of the town, and then lowered the jet onto the makeshift landing pad with little more than a shudder of turbulence.

The cockpit slid open, and Alfonso pulled off helmet and mask in relief.

"Goddamn. You're a good pilot, Sergio, but this is a rough way to travel."

"You'll live, Doc. Don't take long, hear? I've got family in San Luís Potosí. They tell me you're on the trail of a way to stop these dino-dragons. Make it snappy, sir."

They clambered down from the plane and were greeted by the chief of police—who had been three years ahead of Alfonso when he went to the local public schools—and the town mayor, a former lawyer whose hard-nosed approached to crime had made her quite popular in recent years.

"Welcome home, Dr. Becerra," she greeted him warmly. "I'm Mayor Antonia Zavaleta It's unfortunate that such a horrible emergency has brought you back, but we are honored that one of Zongolica's favorite sons is playing such a vital role in combatting the invaders."

"Thanks, Mayor Zavaleta, Chief Corpus," Alfonso put in quickly. "Lieutenant Tinoco will be staying here with you, but I need a lift a little way up the slope here, to the home of Don Pablo Montiel."

"Of course," the chief replied, calling over a pair of officers. "Gentlemen, please drive Dr. Becerra to the destination he indicates."

The ride was short, but Alfonso used it to interrogate his escort about the city.

"Streets are pretty deserted. Where is everyone?"

"Locked up in their homes," said the policeman in the passenger seat, "or hiding in caves in the mountains. There was a bit of a panic this morning, but we got it under control. The major issued an emergency measure closing all but a few key businesses. Just until the crisis passes."

"Anyone hurt? Any real damage?"

The officer shook his head. "No, sir. We locked up some Zetas who were taking advantage of the confusion, and there were a couple of street brawls, but mostly everyone is cooperating. Especially now that the monsters are heading away."

The driver cleared his throat. "Well, it's not as rosy as Gonzalo's making it out to be. People in the caves? They are keeping an eye on Orizaba Peak. If these things emerge from volcanoes, who's to say we won't have one on our doorstep soon?"

Alfonso wished he could reassure them that such a tragedy wouldn't befall them. The only option, however, was to be successful in this quest.

After some five minutes of winding road, the police 4x4 pulled up to Don Pablo's rough-hewn home in the forest. A teenager emerged as Alfonso got out of the car.

"You're Dr. Becerra, right?" the young man said. "He said you'd come."

Nodding, Alfonso asked, "His grandson?"

"Great-grandson. Miguel. He had me send you that text this morning. The dragon-iguana statue or whatever. Says he doesn't understand our 'new-fangled' technology."

They shook hands.

"Well, thanks for that. It helped. He in?"

Miguel opened the door and gestured. "Yes, sir. He's waiting in his study."

The cabin hadn't changed much since Alfonso's father had brought him that very first time as a child. Spartan and clean, with some indigenous weavings and carvings accenting the old, glowing wood. Infused with undeniable spiritual peace.

The study overflowed with books, plants, and sacred stones of various types. Leaning back in a captain's chair sat Don Pablo Montiel, eyes clear despite his eighty years. He nodded at Alfonso and addressed him in Nahuatl.

"A doctor, eh? Filled yourself up with university learning."

"I haven't forgotten my ancestors, Don Pablo, or the traditions you taught me. My work centers on them, with great respect."

"Oh, I know that, son. I've read your articles. Bought your book, too. I can hear the words of the elders echoing in your Spanish lines. Well done."

Alfonso eased onto the rug before the shaman, sat cross-legged as was the custom.

"You sent me that photo. You know what we're up against. These fire wyrms, they're the Lords of the Earth, the ones mentioned in the *Book of Forbidden Songs*. From a letter we discovered, I now know for certain what you have always expected: Sahagún compiled it by binding together the pieces he rejected from the *Cantares Mexicanos*. I think the book might've ended up in Juan Badiano's hands."

The old man leaned forward. "The traditions do tell of a learned Nahua who mastered the ancient tongues of the Castilians. Latin, perhaps is meant. He possessed the book for a time, allowing others to copy it. The original and all the copies, however, have been lost to us down the centuries. As I taught you, in several communities, a few of the songs were kept alive by generations of sacred singers, but even we have begun to forget them."

Swallowing heavily, Alfonso continued. "Okay. This letter between Badiano and Sahagún suggests that there's a spell of some sort that can stop the Lords of the Earth should they emerge. Do you happen to know anything that fits that description?"

Don Pablo was silent for so long that Alfonso worried he hadn't heard the question. Then the old shaman began to scuff his sandled feet in a strange rhythm against the floor. His gnarled and weathered brown hands tapped out a counterpoint on the armrests of his chair.

As suddenly as he'd begun, Don Pablo stopped.

"I've been thinking about it for hours, Alfonso. Dredging up vague memories. A hymn I heard my grandfather sing once, maybe twice: 'Innan in Ahuitzomeh.' Strange, garbled piece."

"'Mother of the Water Dogs,'" Alfonso muttered to himself in Spanish. "Who is she?"

Don Pablo scratched at his scraggly goatee. "Not entirely sure. The hymn calls her Acuetzpalin, suggests she's the mortal enemy of the Lords of the Earth."

Alfonso pulled out his phone, tapped open a recording app.

"Okay. Acuetzpalin. Mother of water dogs—those are the five-handed beasts of legend, right? What else?"

Don Pablo peered up at the ceiling. "As I sought to remember, I realized that this obscure chant had faded from my mind. I never performed it, and as has happened to many sacred singers down the long years, another song was lost to the oral tradition."

Alfonso dropped his head, stared at the phone and his trembling hands. *So close. Where will I go from here? How do I track down another shaman who preserves the songs? There's no time to rush from village to village.*

"Ah," continued Don Pablo, "but my grandfather was no fool. Once I had learned to read and write at school—the first to do so in the long line of sacred singers here in Zongolica, former Tzoncoliuhcan, wind-swept place of twisted hair—he sat me down and sang all the songs he knew, telling me to record them in my halting hand."

In spite of himself, Alfonso felt tears pricking at his eyes. "Oh, by the goddess, Don Pablo ... you transcribed the *Book of Forbidden Songs*?"

The old man's face lit up by degrees, split by a crooked grin. "You bet your ass I did, son. Look behind you on the table."

Alfonso stood with excitement and turned to find an old 1940s school notebook laying open on the rustic surface, its pages yellowed with time, words scrawled in a child's hand in slanting lines. Leaning over, his field experience keeping his hands away to avoid damaging the document, he began to read.

The hymn itself was short, four lines that called out to Acuetzpalin to rise, using multiple worshipful epithets: mother of waterdogs, crusher of wyrms, deposer of the Lords of the Earth.

"Does this read 'ximehua in mictlan?' Rise from the Underworld?"

"Ah, my handwriting was atrocious, apologies. It's 'ximehua in *amictlan*,' or 'rise from the watery depths.' She is the mother of waterdogs, so it makes sense that her resting place would be aquatic."

Pursing his lips a little, Alfonso regarded the rest of the song. It was gibberish, beginning with the sorts of ecstatic shouts that peppered many of these ancient songs—*ahuaya* and the like—before devolving into a string of words the archeologist had never heard before.

"And all this at the end?"

"I'm not certain. It made the piece hard to memorize, of course. Perhaps it's an ancient tongue or secret code. If you show it to other experts, you may uncover something of use."

Suppressing a sigh, Alfonso snapped a photo of the page. "Can you sing it for me? I'd like to record your performance so I can study the hymn more closely."

"Of course. I've been reading it again and again, letting my soul reconnect with the old words and holy rhythms."

Then Don Pablo stood and began to chant, shuffling his feet in complicated steps as he called out to the mysterious foe of fire wyrms.

Alfonso could not help but pray that wherever she was, Acuetzpalin would hear him.

#

Forty-five minutes later, the Harriet Matador was screaming its way over the smoking wreckage of a good chunk of the caravan. Lieutenant Tinoco had gotten word that though Xochitonal had been wounded, it had escaped the blockade and made its way to the city of Santiago de Querétaro, harried the whole way by the survivors of the mission. Alfonso found himself relieved to learn that Elena was still alive and had been blasting at the fire wyrm with the ELF cannon as the team gave chase up Highway 57, threading their precarious way among the interminable line of vehicles fleeing the city.

Following the seeping scar of Xochitonal's rampage into the capital, Tinoco drew the jet up right behind the rear guard of the advancing military forces. As it settled onto the uneven blacktop, the pilot opened the cockpit and sighed.

"Well, Doc, this is where you and me part ways. Sure as hell hope that little trip was worth it. Remember my family and yours, sir. Keep them all safe."

Alfonso now had doubts about his chances, but he kept that to himself as they clambered from the plane. He was fishing about for a reassuring response when he saw Xochitonal's torso towering above the city in the distance. The fire wyrm was hoisting something huge into the air, brick and water crumbling away in orange cascades. As Xochitonal flung the structure at the

American fighter jets that roared around it, Alfonso realized this was the city's unparalleled and towering aqueduct.

A soldier jogged up, drawing Alfonso's eyes away from the devastation.

"Dr. Becerra?"

"Yes. I need to speak to General Navarro."

"He's not available, but I can take you to Dr. Baz. She's on the front line with the ELF cannon."

His stomach queasy, Alfonso rasped a response. "Okay, then. Let's go."

They got into a jeep, and the soldier managed to weave in and out of gouged-up asphalt, shattered cars, and the ruins of buildings that spilled out into the main thoroughfare. Dead bodies sprawled here and there, as did bloody, stinking smears that may have at one time been human beings. The archeologist steeled himself, keeping his eyes on the horror and struggling not to flinch.

Above them, Xochitonal loomed impossibly large, silhouetted against the glitter of twin towers not far beyond it. Alfonso shuddered, thinking of the skyscrapers that had already fallen beneath the titan's inchoate wrath.

They came to the line of troops that was advancing at a steady pace, firing their weapons up at the wyrm, forcing it onward.

"What are they doing?" Alfonso shouted above the din.

"Herding it toward Dr. Baz. She's waiting up ahead with the cannon. Speaking of which, hang on!"

The soldier turned the jeep down an undamaged side street and began to accelerate. After whipping around several corners at breakneck speed, they approached a sort of plaza from the north. The remains of the caravan had set up there—Elena was standing on a low platform, fiddling with controls and shouting orders. Thick black cables snaked from the ELF cannon, leading not to the power source sitting on a sister flatbed, but to a nearby transformer.

She's tapped into the city's electrical grid. What the hell?

Alfonso jumped from the jeep. The ground shuddered beneath his feet. Looking up, he saw Xochitonal crouch and punch its fist through the ground, bellowing in clear challenge.

Running, the archeologist approached the control panel and caught Elena's attention.

"What're you doing?" he called.

She looked at him out of the corner of the eye. "Oh, you're back. We've hurt him. The cannon opens up chinks, exposes him. But then the armor adjusts itself, covers those gaps up. So, since he likes to smash tall buildings, we set up here at the Juriquilla Towers to lure him close. I've knocked him down twice. Needed more juice. Now I think I can put him down for good."

Snapping its massive jaws, Xochitonal surged forward.

Elena gave Alfonso one last glance. "You might want to hold on to something."

Then her hands flew across the keyboard.

A yawing moan bled into the air from the cannon, sliding to a grating whine before going inaudible. The very bones in Alfonso's head vibrated, and though he'd made it through a round trip on the Harrier without getting sick, he now leaned against the frame of the platform and vomited up thin bile.

Because it was crouching, the fire wyrm took the subsonic wave against its head. Alfonso looked up in time to see the chitin moving back from the titan's face, exposing its nauseating features, slimy white skin over an alien, herptile skull. That horrific visage was crisscrossed by ropy red lines—veins or nerves, perhaps.

Xochitonal attempted to right itself. Elena continued to crank the power and modulate frequencies. Glass shattered on buildings behind the fire wyrm. Soldiers in the distance collapsed to the pavement, gripping their heads. The ground trembled like a palsied and dying beast.

The chitin on Xochitonal's chest had receded almost completely, and the exposed and mottled torso—webbed with more of the red cords—wobbled grotesquely as if liable to split open at any moment.

Then, without warning, dozens of similar crimson cables wrapped themselves around the wheels of the flatbed truck bearing the cannon. Alfonso watched dumbfounded and immobile as chunks of alien and shockingly animate chitin anchored themselves to the ground behind the cannon with those same vine-like cords and hauled back, flipping the truck onto its side and tumbling the weapon to the ground.

The stream of powerful frequencies struck the Juriquilla Towers behind him.

With a ghastly screech, the glass blew out on both, showering down like deadly hail.

Elena slapped at the console, shutting off the power.

But there was no stopping it. As Alfonso looked on, unable to move, the buildings buckled and began to fall toward the caravan.

He felt a metallic grip on his shoulder. It was Elena.

"Move, Becerra. Run!"

His legs wouldn't respond. He opened his mouth to gasp or scream, but she just grabbed his arm and yanked him to his feet.

"I said run, goddamn you!"

By then, however, it was too late.

#

Alfonso awakened in the dark. It was hard to breathe. Dust clogged his mouth and the air was close, stale. He was lying on his stomach, it seemed, but when he tried to push himself up, his head bumped against something solid.

Not far away, someone was panting.

"Hello?" he called, whispering for a reason he couldn't explain.

"Becerra?" It was Elena.

"Yeah, it's me. Are you okay?"

She took a ragged breath, as if trying to calm herself. "N-no."

"Oh, hell. You're wounded?" He started to pull himself forward, to try to reach her, but his leg was stuck somehow.

"N-no. I'm ph-physically fine. Just … shit."

There was a long, shaky pause full of shallow gasping.

"Elena?"

"Silvia's dead … Alfonso. It was trying to get to me … then Marco …"

Now she was full-on hyperventilating.

A panic attack. His son had suffered them as a child, triggered by the dark and the silence of the dead of night. Only one thing had ever calmed him.

Softly, Alfonso began to sing Ramiro's favorite song, "I Hope Coffee Rains."

As the strange but soothing lyrics floated on that melody, he could hear the physicist's panting begin to slow. By the time he wrapped up—*so that reality doesn't suffer such pain, in the fields I hope coffee rains*—Elena's breaths were more or less normal.

After a moment of silence, she muttered, "Thank you, Alfonso. You have a nice voice."

"It got me through college. Sang for my supper, as it were. You going to be alright?"

"Yeah. I just got overwhelmed. We're trapped in the rubble. The cannon's probably damaged. And ... I don't do well in dark, enclosed spaces."

Like most Mexicans their age, Alfonso knew the reason. Even in Zongolica, it had been the only topic of conversation for days when he was in second grade: the six-year-old daughter of the Secretary of Foreign Affairs had been kidnapped by a gang called the Hyenas. After being held hostage for more than a month, she had finally been rescued by a Special Forces team.

The kidnappers had amputated her arm as a proof of life.

"That's ... understandable. It may be hard for you to believe, given the conflicts we've had, but I've always admired your resilience, you know. It couldn't have been easy, overcoming something like that, even with a wealthy family."

She made a scoffing noise. "Yeah, well, most people don't know this, but they asked for a ransom right off the bat. Something my parents could've paid without too much trouble. It would've hurt them some, but it was doable. But my father ... he decided he wasn't going to negotiate with them. Said they would just gouge him for more later. The authorities would find the criminals, he insisted. God's hand would guide them."

"No freaking way, Elena." Alfonso tried to imagine his own son being abducted. He would have paid anything, *done* anything, to get Ramiro back.

"And my mother, she just went along with his plan. Didn't fight him. Didn't demand he bring her little girl back right then."

A sob echoed quietly in the small space. Alfonso knew not to speak, to just listen and understand.

"The Hyenas were *rabid*. Pissed beyond words. Their leader growled something about proof of life, and then they held me down while he lifted this filthy machete ..."

It was too much for her. She wept for several minutes there in the dark, just a meter or so away. Alfonso couldn't comfort her. Even if he hadn't been stuck, he suspected she wouldn't have wanted his pity.

Soon, though, she sniffed the worst of it away. "I'm not oblivious, Alfonso. I know what people think about me. About my privilege, the money, my light skin and hair, these blue eyes that our twisted Mexican sensibilities value so much. Most people don't see the scientist, the military advisor, the woman who struck out on her own when her parents fled the country. To them, I'm the Bionic Barbie, the pretty little girl who was rescued from the predators and grew up into a symbol."

"You're not wrong," he replied when she paused, "though plenty of us respect you—if from a distance."

Her chuckle was ironic. "Here's the real reason my father didn't pay the ransom, even if he never will admit it. I was born with a defect. Radial Dysplasia, it's called. A club hand. My father was always embarrassed by it, blamed my mother. It's why they never had another child. When the Hyenas severed that source of shame, mailed it to him, he finally broke down and asked the President to send the Special Forces Corps after me."

Breath hissed through Alfonso's teeth, and before he could stop himself, he growled, "Bastard."

"Yeah, that he is."

"I'm sorry, Elena. Sorry you went through all that shit and sorry I added to it with my tactless snark."

"Ah, it's okay. I've been a real bitch to you. I'm surprised at your decency, all things considered."

They sat without speaking for another minute or so. It was an oddly comfortable silence, the kind that comes from getting past long-standing conflict.

At last, Elena sighed.

"But enough with my depressing life. How about you? Any loved ones you're keeping an eye on in all this madness?"

"Well, I come from a typical indigenous mountain family—working class, half-dozen kids. I was the oldest and first to go to college in the family, but my brothers and sisters have pretty much followed in my footsteps, though they've stayed in that area. A couple of them are teachers and engineers, etc. I have a son, Ramiro—he lives with my ex-wife in Reynosa."

"Ah. Is she from the border originally? How you'd two meet?"

"It's kind of goofy, really. I was coming back from a dig in Oaxaca, riding the bus, and she was sitting next to me. Had been visiting friends on the coast. We struck up a conversation—she'd never been to Mexico City, and when we stopped, she stuck around for a few days instead of taking the next leg of her journey back home. I showed her the sights, and well, one thing led to another. But we really didn't know each other, and even with Ramiro, the marriage started to crumble after a few years."

A faint rasping sound filled the narrow space when he fell silent.

"Sounds like they're looking for us," Elena said.

"Yeah, that's a relief."

The darkness was lit up without warning. A phone was lying not far from Alfonso. He reached out and picked it up.

"Thank God. It's my smart phone. Contains important new information I need to share with you."

He held up the device, activating the flashlight. Elena was huddled a meter or so away, hugging her knees, head bent under the structural beam that had kept the weight of the rubble off of them both. At that moment, vulnerable yet strong, she was more beautiful than ever. He bit his lip in surprise at the surge of emotions.

Blinking and holding up her bionic hand to block the light, she asked, "Missed call?"

"Yeah." He tried calling back, but the circuits were busy. "Probably General Navarro."

"I'm sure it is. Marco won't stop until he's dug me out. But it's going to take a while, I'm betting." She gave a bitter laugh, leaning forward and pressing her fist into the blacktop beneath them. "Alright, Alfonso. Now that I've gone and killed who-knows-how-many people, time to admit I was wrong. The cannon is probably destroyed or damaged. So let's talk back-up plan. What's this new information you've got for me?"

Smiling, he tapped his phone, bringing up the photo of Acuetzpalin's hymn.

"For starters, I think we need to lure the fire wyrms to the Gulf of Mexico."

CHAPTER ELEVEN: MARCO

"It's a goddamn miracle."

His adrenaline surging, Marco turned away from excoriating the Special Forces Corps unit to face Brigadier General Felipe Gonzales, the squat, mustachioed man who had operational command in Military Region XII at the moment.

"What, did we find them?"

Gonzales squinted for a second as if trying to understand. "Ah. No, not yet, though we've detected two heat signatures in the area you indicated. I'm referring to the ELF cannon. It sustained some minor damage, but it appears to be largely intact."

Relieved to hear that there were signs of life, Marco looked out from the command tent over the ruins of the Juriquilla Towers. Most of the heavy equipment and men crawled over the one smoking wreck of twisted metal that had collapsed atop the cannon and its crew, including Elena Baz and Alfonso Becerra. In the distance, he could make out the receding form of Xochitonal, slowed but still rampaging toward the north as jet planes harried him.

"Get out there," the general snapped at the COIFEs, "and help them dig her out. You'd better pray to God she's not badly hurt."

The soldiers saluted him and double-timed out to the wreckage. Marco clenched his fists to suppress his indignation at them and his own feelings of powerlessness. When he had seen the towers tumbling toward Elena, his heart had nearly broken.

So many years of keeping her safe, of ensuring her place in the world, only to see her crushed beneath that glass and steel ...

But he hadn't given up. That lesson she had taught him as well. To endure what was impossible to endure.

Now, as the crews struggled to extract what they could from the shattered buildings, he and Brigadier General Gonzales reviewed the advance of Sipakna, which was presently smashing its way through San Juan de los Lagos in Jalisco state. In response to what it saw as the President's incompetence in dealing with the organisms, the New Generation Jalisco Cartel was threatening to take matters into its own hands.

"Enough innocent lives have been lost because of this fool!" their communique declared. "Reporters, teachers, students: obviously all that blood wasn't enough for Mr. Chupacabras and his American collaborators! But we have something in our possession that will end the monsters once and for all, and we've got the balls to use it!"

In the midst of the generals' strategic planning with other command staff, the whirring of helicopter blades drew them out of the tent. A US military Osprey was setting down just beyond the devastation. As Mexican troops rushed to meet them, two dozen officers and soldiers exited the tiltrotor transport. Marco sighed. He'd been expecting their arrival, but it didn't make things any easier.

After an exchange, the newcomers were escorted to the command tent. A tall, bald officer—clearly Latino—saluted the Mexican generals.

"Gentlemen," he announced in Spanish, "As you know, your president has authorized a team to be embedded within every region affected or under threat by the hostile organisms. I'm Colonel Ron Acosta, the US military advisor assigned to Region XII."

"Welcome," Gonzales replied. "I'm Brigadier General Felipe Gonzales, local operational commander, and this is Marco Navarro, division general for Region I. We were just reviewing the progress of Sipakna, the other fire wyrm, while our teams dig out the ELF cannon and a couple of scientists who survived the collapse of these buildings. If you'll come inside, we'll get you up to speed."

Acosta gave commands to his team, deploying some to aid with coordinating rescue efforts and bringing others inside with them.

Marco laid the trajectory of each fire wyrm out on a screen, and the American colonel nodded.

"Our experts were predicting that the creatures would rendezvous at a point near San Luís Potosí, and that definitely appears to be the case. On the way over, I reviewed footage from the disastrous encounter here. Though your team has clearly uncovered weaknesses in the hostiles, you've been less successful in exploiting those. The force required to compromise their exoskeleton is too destructive to allow other weapons to take advantage of those gaps."

Marco lifted a cautious finger. "Perhaps. Our top scientists have been examining a large piece of chitin that dislodged itself and autonomously attacked the ELF cannon, bringing about the fall of the Juriquilla Towers. We're due for an update from them; let me have them sent for."

Nodding at one of the aides present, the general sent him rushing off toward the mobile laboratory.

"Our scientists back in the States," continued Acosta, "theorize that the two hostiles are meeting up to mate. I can't emphasize enough how cataclysmic it would be for that to happen. At all costs, we must keep the creatures apart."

"All costs?" Gonzales asked.

"Our government has been pressing for a nuclear strike, urging your President to have the two hostiles lured into the remoter areas of Zacatecas state so that we can launch an ICBM against them. Casualty estimates from fallout are well below what experts calculate will be the death toll if the threat isn't dealt with soon. In any event, Congress just approved a measure authorizing the use of extreme force should these organisms come within 200 kilometers of the border."

Marco's eyebrow went up. "So if they were to move farther north than Monterrey, the US is willing to drop a bomb on an ally?"

"Beyond a doubt, General Navarro. Understand the panic that has spread across America. Add to that the negative public sentiment toward Mexico…"

"Yes," Marco interrupted, "we watched your most recent presidential election. We're acutely aware of the vitriol hurled against us."

"Then you'll see the impetus for this decision. Trust me, international sentiment is behind us as well, with both Russia and China giving their public support for American intervention. So the choice has become simple. Either your leadership enlists our help to stop the invaders ASAP, or we will take unilateral action."

Before either Marco or Felipe could respond, Astrid Estrada burst into the tent, hair awry and eyes wide. In her wake came Roberto Menchaca, who had long ago dispensed with his suit coat and tie and now wore a lab coat over a Kevlar vest.

"Generals," Astrid said, nodding at everyone in the room. "You wanted an update?"

"Please, Dr. Estrada. This is Colonel Acosta, with the US Armed Forces. He's our new advisor."

"Hey, there," the biologist greeted in English as Robert accessed a portable terminal in the tent. "Okay, so we've only had about a half hour with what we would've once called a chunk of the fire wyrm's armor, but we've learned a few things. First, the chitin is actually made up of hundreds of thousands of interconnected organisms which together form a symbiote—a sort of beneficial parasite for the host organism beneath it."

Robert pulled up an image of the irregular-shaped hunk of iridescent blue. "One obvious function is protection—the external crystalline shell is nanostructured in a stunning way, making it virtually indestructible by conventional weapons. As a result, following Dr. Becerra's fashion of using Nahuatl names for the wyrms, we're calling them *chimaltontli*. Little shields."

On the screen, a team slowly flipped the fragment, revealing a fleshier underbelly from which a half-dozen red tendrils blossomed among strange orifices and organs.

"These appendages," Astrid said, gesturing at the screen, "have a hybrid function. They connect the chimaltontli together, transferring information and unusual nutrients with a metal-oxide and silicate base. They can also serve as tentacles."

One of the nerve-tendrils moved sluggishly on the monitor, as if trying even in death to grab one of the laboratory assistants.

"The other structures you see here benefit the host organism by regulating air pressure and processing our atmospheric gasses into noxious fumes that the fire wyrms can breathe."

Roberto rasped a harsh laugh. "The stench is insane, even with masks on."

Marco studied the images for a moment before speaking. "Any luck with a chemical compound that can compromise the ... chimaltontli?"

"Uh, no. Their outer shell is tougher than anything on this planet. The pressures and temperatures you'd need to crack through them are ... pretty much unfeasible."

"A thermonuclear explosion would do the trick, though, wouldn't it?" asked Acosta.

Roberto arched an eyebrow. "Well, clearly."

Astrid jumped in. "But in reality we just need to figure out how to pry away enough of the chimaltontli for long enough that a powerful conventional weapon can pierce the exposed flesh of the wyrm."

Several simultaneous conversations broke out about the merits of one approach over the other. In the midst of the tension, an aid called Brigadier General Gonzales aside to confer with him.

"The teams have broken through to Drs. Baz and Becerra," he announced to everyone, stilling the debate. "Both of them are fine. They should be fully extracted in a few minutes."

Astrid sighed with relief. "Finally some good news."

The tension in Marco eased at the news. For the better part of an hour, he'd been on tenterhooks, trying not to think about the possibility Elena had been killed. Even when speaking with his daughters to reassure them he was fine, he couldn't stop fretting like a father for her wellbeing. That bond, forged of pain and vengeance and respect, at times felt stronger than blood or love. Her absence from the world, even though they only spoke a few times a year, was unthinkable to him.

Stepping outside the command tent to watch the extraction from afar, Marco caught a flash of light out of the corner of his eye. As he turned, smoke curled into a bruised fist of black and yellow on the horizon. The sound of the explosion reached his ears then, as the ground rumbled beneath his feet.

The others rushed out, exclaiming in shock. Marco turned to Colonel Acosta.

"Tell me this wasn't you."

The American gave a slight shake of his head. "No. And it looks conventional, not nuclear."

Everyone scrambled for data. Drones and pilots confirmed satellite imagery: a car bomb had been driven at Xochitonal, exploding at its feet on the edges of the city.

The Jalisco New Generation Cartel was claiming responsibility for the attack. "Since no one else had the balls to use a nuke," they said on their YouTube channel, "we went ahead and stepped up."

The problem was, Marco soon learned, that the assholes hadn't used a nuclear weapon.

They'd put a dirty bomb in that car. Xochitonal had shrugged the explosion off like every other conventional measure.

The radiation, however, was sweeping south over Santiago de Querétaro, a slow and deadly haze endangering the lives of people who hadn't evacuated or died in the fire wyrm's path.

CHAPTER TWELVE: CHARLOTTE

August 16, 1938—

We set off as soon as I'd given Captain Maldonado the money and stowed my things in the cabin he assigned me. I both appreciated and was unnerved by his general announcement to the men that I was not to be disturbed or accosted in any way—the cost of any untoward behavior would be *all* their wages. Many of the crew are new, so a good chunk of the day has been spent sorting the niceties of duties and shifts.

Throughout the day, I would peer from time to time behind us with the captain's eyeglass. Several ships have joined the hunt, but we have the advantage of seasoned, hardened men who are used to weeks upon the waves. I can't imagine the softer crème de la crème of deep South Texas stands much of a chance against my team.

On repeated occasions, the captain informed me that my husband is sending requests by Coast Guard radio that I get in contact with him immediately. I ignored and will continue to ignore him. Let him fret and worry like the weak Biblical helpmate he must yearn for in secret.

By early afternoon, the horizon had become a broad circle of water that blurred into sky, a bowl of blue upon blue, dotted with white above and below. The call of men and the call of gulls merged in my ear. The hum of the motor and the thrum of the waves a single, primal plainsong.

Now, near dusk, we have seen nothing of note, though Captain Maldonado assures me we've drawn close to area where the creature was last sighted. The wind has begun to pick up, scudding fiery clouds into the sunset. I smile at the ferocity of the ocean as its waves stir beneath that glancing touch of a warm, Caribbean *sharqi*—the wet and briny air scintillates with almost erotic energy as the first stars wink in gleaming conspiracy from above.

In my fancy, I'm a midwife, preparing to ease the creature born to wind and wave from the dark, unsoundable depths.

August 17, 1938—

Early this morning we came upon the wreckage of a fishing boat, strewn across the whitecaps like driftwood or kindling. We began to cross the area with great care, lookouts scrutinizing every possible angle.

Some hours into this search, the American boats arrived, the *Andrey* at point. Burnell brought his yacht alongside the *Doña Angélica* and waved at me.

"Your man's looking for you, Miss Charlotte," he called.

"I don't have a *man*," I retorted. "I have a husband, and he can damn well wait till I'm done. In the meantime, I suggest you get the hell out of my way, Mr. Burnell."

He went red as a beet while the men on board his ship burst into laughter.

"Alright, gal, but you ought not be out here. Lots of witnesses to my warning—you're going to get yourself killed, and those Mexicans, too."

His pilot steered clear of us, and just about everyone kept their distance after that. The wind stilled as fishermen on each boat scanned the shattered timbers for signs of the predator. Crews tossed chum onto the low swells, hoping to lure it to the surface.

But no one caught any sight of the monster.

Now the chop on the Gulf is getting rougher as night falls. Some of the ships have spotlights they've begun to point at the burgundy depths.

I suspect so much commotion has driven the creature many fathoms beneath us.

August 18, 1938—

I was nearly spilled from my cot by a sudden swell this morning. The sea has been stirred to anger by all the pieces of shit currently floating upon her immaculate surface. Battered by the waves, burning up more fuel than they'd anticipated, two ships from the rag-tag masculine expedition have turned tail and headed back to port.

The *Andrey* remains, of course. Burnell's pilot continues to crisscross the shattered remains of the old fishing boat, to no avail. I can almost imagine the old son of a bitch, railing against women who don't know their place and the uppity Mexicans who help them.

Captain Maldonado says that farther southeast there have been other sightings, incidents never shared with the American authorities, out over international waters.

I ask whether we can move that way under stealthy cover of darkness. He agrees.

I imagine Burnell's face in the morning. The vision makes me laugh.

August 19, 1938—

It has taken us most of the day to reach the coordinates. I cannot sleep. I sit here, near the prow, my feet propped on the gunwale, scanning the waves.

I'm a patient woman. Learned it from my father.

"The water doesn't reward folks who get too anxious or greedy," he used to whisper as we sat upon a lake, mist lapping the banks like some lazy amorphous god. "You have to sit still, empty of thought, utterly open. Don't try to force it. Don't try to impose your will. Simply wait for the water's gift, Charlotte."

Yes, Father. I'm waiting.

August 20, 1938—

A young Lothario, heedless of the captain's warning, approached me this morning.

Most of the men on the *Doña Angélica* are either married or green adolescents. There are a few single fellows with a hungry glint in their eye, and one of these—Gonzalo, I think he's called—

sidled up to me with a leering proposition that even my poor ability with Spanish could easily make out.

Smirking at him, I bent to my tackle box and withdrew my razor-sharp scaling knife, pointing it at his nether regions.

"Unless you're looking to be castrated, sir, I suggest you go about your duties."

He scoffed, muttering curses, but he went away. Several of his shipmates witnessed the exchange and told the captain, who assures me Gonzalo has been given a stern talking to. I'm not certain I trust men's mutual policing of their impulses, however, so I'm wearing the knife on a sheath at my waist from here on out.

I'm back in my cabin after another fruitless day. The waves rock me hard, a desperate mother furious I won't sleep. All day the sea has been swelling, perhaps unable to contain whatever leviathan struggles to escape me. The captain says a storm must be swirling far to the south.

Still, nothing. Marlin, flashing bright against a cloud-streamered sky. Dolphins, chattering their amicable hullo. The whetted edge of the wind, seeking to bar our way. The sullen sea, knowing I mean to wrest her child from her liquid embrace.

Ah, waxing poetic again. It's not all my fault. My father loved books and stories about fishing and whaling, read to me from *Moby Dick* and Jack London's *Tales of the Fish Patrol*, among others. Charles often shares stories with me about the sea, indulging my passion with literary bits. I love to hear his voice, though if I'm honest; it pales by comparison with the harmonies of wind and wave.

What was it that Byron said? "There is society where none intrudes, by the deep sea, and music in its roar."

There's a poem, by Longfellow. I remembered a scrap of it just now, the wind twisting like a sunburned and jealous lover through my hair.

> My soul is full of longing
> for the secret of the sea,
> and the heart of the great ocean
> sends a thrilling pulse through me.

Come now, Old Mother. Give up your secret. I promise I'll be gentle.

August 21, 1938—
The bitch is mocking me. She is ancient and canny, the sea. Freighted with eons, older than mountains or canyons, ever-flowing source of life and abrupt bringer of death.

Awful stirrings that draw me to my feet, leaning out over that formlessness. What grim divinity undulates so very far below? Carlos says his ancestors worshipped the Gulf as a goddess whose name has been lost to the Huasteca, his people. He speaks of human sacrifice before the arrival of the Spanish, and I think of all the sunken ships since. A watery potter's field at the bottom, yes. All over-grown with coral and sea grass, dim except when briefly lit by an errant beam of clinquant sun that wavers sickly to the ocean floor.

Perhaps the shades of those lost men and women make up the nameless goddess, the hungry conglomeration of dead that lie dreaming below. Stirred by reveries of life they churn within their barnacled graves, sending restless currents surging to the surface.

Enough of this. Maldonado wants to turn back. I ask for two more days. He reluctantly agrees.

August 21, 1938—
What on Earth possessed me to attempt this madness? I can barely stomach the thought of returning. The looks of pity alone are liable to drive me to homicide.

Why on Earth... Oh! Why call this planet Earth? She is all ocean and lake and river. The Huasteca worshipped the Gulf as a goddess. And the river and the sea are one, a single entity forever flowing through my grasp in laughing streams. Like piss, useless and shameful.

#

At last! I was ready to throw this goddamned journal in the water and turn the *Doña Angélica* around, but a shrimper came up over the horizon and signaled us.

Their crew was frantic, the captain desperate to get back to Tampico.

They saw it. The monster. It stole their catch not twelve hours ago.

LORDS OF THE EARTH

CHAPTER THIRTEEN: ELENA

Elena had no time to look for Marco and confer with him. No sooner had she and Alfonso emerged from the rubble than a soldier thrust bottles of water in their hands and hurried them toward a large transport helicopter.

"Sorry, ma'am," he said over her objections. "There's not a lot of time for explanations, and the general is already pissed beyond reason. We need to evacuate you and the other surviving members of the team ASAP."

"Will the general be joining us?" Alfonso asked, replacing the cap on his bottle.

"At the rendezvous point, yes, sir."

Accepting circumstances for what they were, Elena ducked her head as they neared the helicopter and climbed inside. Roberto and Astrid were already strapped in, along with a half dozen other technicians and specialists.

"What's going on?" Elena asked, raising her voice to be heard above the roar of the rotors.

"The idiot cartel used a dirty bomb against Xochitonal," Roberto explained with an exaggerated roll of his eyes. "It obviously had no effect other than to spread fallout. So we're flying around it, meeting up with the troops on the outskirts of Santa María del Río."

Elena tried to remember the geography of the region. "That's just south of San Luís Potosí, isn't it?"

Astrid lifted her tablet, displaying a map. "Yeah. Xochitonal's making a mad dash in that direction. So is Sipakna. Best bet? They're looking to hook up. The Americans are afraid they'll mate and have a bunch of little fire wyrmies. It's a strong possibility, I have to concede."

"The Americans?" Elena knew they had been conferring with the President, but this sounded like a new development.

"Yes," Roberto answered. "They've embedded advisors in the military regions likely to be impacted by the First and Second Emergence, along with places where other volcanoes could give rise to more of the creatures."

Astrid leaned forward, raising an eyebrow. "They are pushing to nuke our two not-so-friendly Lords of the Earth."

"And threatening to do so if they get too close to the border," Roberto added.

Elena glanced over at Alfonso, who was staring out the window as the helicopter rose into the air. His cheek was glistening with tears.

"What?" she asked, laying her hand on his. It was a gesture she would have scoffed at two hours ago, but the archeologist had shown such compassion to her there beneath the rubble, without a bit of condescension. She found herself beginning to care for him despite their rocky professional past, despite some of his harebrained ideas.

Alfonso made a weak gesture at the window. "They just pulled a plane from the rubble. It's the one that took me to Zongolica and back. The pilot was … His name was Sergio Tinoco. Good guy. He has family in San Luís Potosí. Made me promise … ah, shit."

She squeezed Alfonso's hand as he stifled a sob. "It's okay. We've got a plan. Let's just get to the rendezvous point and explain everything to Marco."

He wiped his eyes, dropped his other hand over hers in silent agreement.

Turning to Astrid and Roberto, she asked, "Were they able to recover the ELF cannon?"

"Yeah. They're transporting it to Santa María del Río," Astrid explained.

"The idea being," Roberto continued, "to make once last go of it before the Americans take the reins. Though, based on our findings, I'm not sure we've got many options left to us."

Brushing dust from her pants, Elena leaned back. The helicopter shuddered slightly with some turbulence. Below them, in the distance, Xochitonal was making his inexorable way north, head bent with inscrutable determination.

"Sounds grim. But there's always something, guys. Even in the darkest moments, if you hold on a little longer, another way might reveal itself. Tell us what you've learned about the fire wyrms. Then Alfonso will map out our plan."

Eyes wide with apparent surprise at this statement of hope, Astrid started explaining.

#

Less than a half hour later, the helicopter settled down just outside of Santa María del Río, a small city perched on the Mesa del Centro at the western edge of the Sierra Madre Oriental. The team emerged and were escorted by soldiers to the bustling staging area, where other helicopters and trucks were dropping off equipment to be assembled on site.

As they walked, Astrid stepped close to Elena and addressed her at a volume that wouldn't be overheard.

"So, you and Alfonso …"

Elena looked over at her with a suspicious lift of an eyebrow. "Me and Alfonso what?"

"Well, what happened between you two while you were trapped?"

"What do you mean? Nothing, Astrid. We talked about the plan and waited for rescue."

"Alright, if it's too personal, fine. I know you and I aren't really friends or anything, and your love of privacy is pretty notorious."

Elena caught the younger biologist's arm as she began to walk off.

"Hey, wait. What are you getting at?"

"Hello. It's obvious you two like each other. A lot."

Elena was taken aback, at a loss for words. "What?"

"I mean, there was already some tension there before. Physical attraction, maybe. But now? You comforted him on the helicopter, Elena. You looked downright *concerned* about him. And, holy shit, did he light up when you put your hand on his."

Searching for a retort, the physicist just shook her head. "You're imagining things. Besides, this is hardly the time for romance, wouldn't you say?"

They had reached the staging area by that point, so Elena was spared any further speculation by her younger colleague as everyone caught up and they were ushered into a tent to await the command staff.

Elena gave Alfonso a furtive glance. She found him attractive, sure, though she had a good four centimeters on him. And he had shown kindness to her, unblemished by mockery or irony. But she also understood how tragedy heightens the emotions, draws people together in unnatural ways. Even if she didn't have pressing responsibilities to the country as a whole to consider, she would have been very cautious about acting on her feelings under such circumstances.

Marco entered after a few minutes, accompanied by aides.

"So, Elena, they tell me you have important intel. What've you figured out?"

"The short version is that we need to lure the fire wyrms to the coast. Alfonso has discovered that pre-Colombian peoples defeated them in the past with the help of some sort of aquatic organism. Our working hypothesis is that the First and Second Emergence have stirred it into action again, hence the sudden advent of this hurricane."

Marco gave her an odd, incredulous look. "That's ... pretty thin, Elena. And the Americans are quite anxious right now. I can't imagine they—or the President—will readily accept the risk of drawing these monsters across the country in hopes that something's going to rise from the Gulf and defeat them for us."

Roberto cleared his throat. "Told you guys."

Elena felt a rush of adrenaline. "Marco ... General ... this is your research team, unanimous, setting aside all differences, recommending a course of action. You're seriously going to ignore our advice?"

Marco made a frustrated gesture in the air. "I don't want to, Elena, but this option you're giving me ... just isn't an option. How would you lure them, anyway?"

"Using the ELF cannon. I can tweak the programming to imitate their calls."

The general blanched. "There's no way they'll let me take our only non-nuclear weapon and use it as bait, people. Listen, right now there are international pressures coming to bear. We have no choice at the moment but to stop Xochitonal in its tracks *here*, in Santa María del Río."

Elena growled with frustration. "So, what, the third time's the charm?"

Astrid interjected, "Because this organism isn't some instinct-driven beast, General. It is pretty clearly sentient, with a definite understanding of who we are and what we're attempting. *It went after Elena.* Can recognize her and her role in this fight. Do you truly think it will just walk up to the cannon again and allow us to attack it?"

Before Marco could respond, the American contingent swept in. Elena noted right away the tall, bald Mexican-American the others had told her ran the embed. Ron Acosta.

"Is your team ready?"

"Jesus Christ," Alfonso muttered in disgust. "They barely dragged her out of the rubble, and you guys already want her to face that bastard again?"

"We don't have the luxury of downtime, sir." Acosta's face betrayed no regret or humor. "This may be your country's last chance to deal with the organisms on your own terms."

Elena felt a shivery epiphany rush over her. Their next step became clear. Touching Alfonso's arm in warning before he said anything else, she nodded. "Fine. I'm going. What's Xochitonal's ETA?"

"About twenty minutes," Marco informed her. "Your technicians are setting everything up."

"Good. I'll need my colleagues with me if that's okay."

"Of course," the general rasped with a shaky nod. "Anything you require, just ask."

As they were escorted toward the weapon, Alfonso leaned in close. "What the hell, Elena? Are you really going to expose yourself to it again?"

"Look, guys, we need the technicians on our side. I've got to talk to them, and I want you to keep the soldiers occupied so they don't overhear."

Roberto adjusted the straps of his flak jacket. "Why? What's your plan?"

Glancing around at their escort, she whispered hoarsely.

"We're going to steal the ELF cannon from the Army and do this ourselves."

#

Minutes sped by in breathless jerks. By the time Marco joined her at the control terminal, Elena had gotten key people to agree to help; others had given assurances as to their silence. Those who were forever loyal to the Army didn't catch wind of the plot taking shape.

All that remained was to survive the next few minutes.

The staging area was partly encircled by woods, and Elena was the first to notice how the branches of the mulberry trees had begun to sway.

"It's coming," she told Marco, and he radioed his aides.

Commands were relayed up and down the line. Batteries of ground-to-air missiles swiveled in readiness. Helicopters lifted into the air behind them. American jets swooped around, preparing for the needed opening.

The vibrations in the ground steadily increased in force until they shook everything with violent abandon.

"Something's wrong!" Astrid shouted from behind the protective cordon. "This doesn't make sense!"

"What was that?" Marco demanded of the command staff, his finger tapping the earpiece. "Oh, shit. Elena…it's *running* toward us!"

The physicist didn't hesitate. Even though the fire wyrm had not come into view, she slapped the beam awake, blasting at the forest, denuding trees and then ripping them to kindling.

Then they all saw it. The ancient monster was rushing at them through the woods, head down, eyes full of rage.

Just before it entered the ELF cannon's range of fire, it leapt into the air. The force of its push-off from the ground sent a tremor through the staging area, tumbling personnel and materiel to the dirt. As Xochitonal sailed like some infernal zeppelin overhead, blocking the afternoon sun for a second, Elena shut off the beam and turned to Marco.

"We're screwed," she muttered, eyes wide, heart pounding.

The general grabbed her and rushed her down the steps of the platform. The military fired frantic missiles at the behemoth, to no avail. Then, raining down from the fire wyrm, came dozens upon dozens of chimaltontli, nerve tendrils lashing out, adhering to or wrapping around vehicles, weapons, people. One whipped its way in seconds to the terminal, using its tendrils as zip lines to speed from one anchor point to another with deadly speed.

Soldiers opened fire, but the chitin fragments turned their armored sides toward the attacks and were unharmed. One flung a tendril around a COIFE's legs, then another around his torso, and twisted, ripping him in half in an explosion of gore.

Xochitonal landed hundreds of meters away, the impact flipping vehicles and sending Elena sprawling. Marco stumbled but remained upright, stooping to help Elena. Ignoring the scrapes and incipient bruises, she clambered back to her feet and kept running.

Soon they reached the other scientists, who were crouching at the center of a circle of guards.

"We need to get these people out of here," Marco shouted, "now! To the jeeps—hurry!"

The group made its way to a cluster of vehicles, the guards attempting to keep chimaltontli at bay with suppressive fire.

Tendrils managed to snap toward them all the same. A soldier had his legs shorn off in a bright blossom of blood. Another was decapitated.

The COIFE in front of Elena screamed as his arm was ripped off. The xiuhcoatl rifle he had been carrying dropped to the ground, and Elena scooped it up by instinct.

They reached the jeeps, the four scientists scrambling into the one Marco indicated as he got behind the wheel. The remaining soldiers got into the other jeeps, forming a protective shield around the center jeep as the frantic convoy jerked into motion.

But the chimaltontli kept coming. The road was lined with trees, and those chitin fragments swung from bole to bole, from branch to branch. Soldiers began to fire at them from the moving vehicles, trying to slow them down. But their speed soon matched that of the transports, allowing them to hurl themselves in attack.

A chimaltontli slammed against the jeep, grabbing hold of the vehicle on Alfonso's side.

Adrenaline surged in Elena's breast.

"Get down!" she screamed.

As Alfonso ducked, she began firing at the thing with the xiuhcoatl she had retrieved. Years of practice under Marco's supervision had inured her to the kick against her shoulder. Round after round she unloaded into the softer underbelly of the creature, tearing into those horrific organs. Foul sulfuric gore spattered her clothes and Alfonso's back, but she kept shooting till the clip was empty.

Several tentacles fell away from the chimaltontli, useless, but it still clung with vicious tenacity to the jeep. Marco swiveled in his seat, trying to both drive at breakneck speeds and fire his pistol at the parasite.

Ignoring him, fueled by rage and fear, Elena started bludgeoning the chimaltontli with the butt of the assault rifle. One of the remaining tendrils ripped the gun from her hands, pulling her forward till she was almost kneeling on Alfonso's back, the ruined remains of that inscrutable alien belly just inches from her face.

With a scream of frustration, Elena clenched her bionic hand into a fist and began to pummel the slick flesh with punch after punch.

"Get! The! Fuck! Off! This! Jeep!" she cried, punctuating every word with a blow.

Then a tendril coiled quick around her myoelectric arm and squeezed, shattering it and ripping it from her body, nearly dislocating her shoulder with the force.

Elena tumbled back against Roberto, eyes filling with tears of bitter frustration and impotence. In the front, Astrid had managed to slide into the driver's seat while Marco stood and fired rounds into the remaining tentacles before kicking the chimaltontli free of the jeep at last.

"Holy shit!" Roberto exclaimed, his voice cracking, as Elena righted herself.

Alfonso straightened and immediately reached for her, worry clouding his eyes as he saw the jagged bits of wire, plastic and metal that hung from the stump of her arm.

Nausea churned in Elena's stomach as he regarded her. The last thing she needed was for him to feel sorry for her.

Covering the remains of her prosthesis with her only hand, she shook her head.

"Don't look at me like that. I can't bear it."

"Like what?"

"With pity in your eyes."

Thrusting his lank black hair back with a trembling hand, he sighed.

"No way. This isn't pity. It's awe. You're a freaking bad-ass, Elena Baz."

Relief spread its way through her chest, and the edges of her lips began to turn up into a smile.

Then Astrid screamed, swerving to avoid another chimaltontli.

The jeep came up off its passenger-side wheels and began to flip.

CHAPTER FOURTEEN: ALFONSO

Alfonso regained consciousness, his ears ringing. He was face-down in the grass on the side of the road. Pushing himself unsteadily up with his arms, he glanced around. The jeep was lying on its side not far away. Roberto was standing beside it, pulling Astrid free through the shattered windshield.

The sound of gunfire pulled Alfonso completely to his feet. It was Marco, a few meters from the flipped vehicle, limping toward several chimaltontli in the treeline.

Turning back to the jeep, Alfonso saw Elena, struggling to climb out with just one hand. He rushed over, climbed up onto the jeep, just as their escort came back around for them after, having overshot the wreck.

"Here, give me your hand," Alfonso called down to Elena, reaching for her. She gripped his forearm to give him more leverage, and together they extricated her from the overturned vehicle.

Beside her missing arm and some bruises, the physicist appeared unharmed. His chest constricted at the sight of her. In a shock of emotional revelation, Alfonso realized how much she meant to him now. He had always found her brilliant and beautiful, but what drew him to her was this amazing strength, resilience, tenacity.

They exchanged a portentous look for several seconds there atop the jeep. Soldiers were fanning out around them, helping the general fend off the chitin fragments.

Directly below them, Roberto had finally extricated Astrid, who was clearly in bad shape.

"Help me get her to a jeep!" he shouted at a nearby soldier. "She needs medical attention ASAP!"

Just then, a tendril shot from the nearby trees, seizing Roberto around the waist. The approaching soldier began to fire, trying to sever the alien appendage.

"Oh, holy hell," Roberto gurgled, blood dribbling from his lips.

In a sickening twist, the tendril squeezed and ripped the chemical engineer in two, splattering gore all over Astrid. She began to scream hoarsely despite her wounds. The tentacle whipped back toward the woods, yanking Roberto's torso with it through the air, his intestines unraveling like some bloody extension of its length.

"Mother of God," Alfonso muttered, numbed by shock. "Shit, we need to get down, quick."

Elena nodded wordlessly, her face slack with grief.

Clambering down the back, Alfonso helped her descend. Soldiers rushed them to a jeep. Marco and Astrid were loaded into another, and the vehicles tore down the road at a madcap pace as a plane passed overhead and bombed the forest into a blaze of oblivion.

As he stared into Elena's glassy, distant eyes, Alfonso prayed that the horrible screeching sounds emerging from the conflagration were the death rattles of the chimaltontli. She desperately needed a respite from tragedy. They all did.

#

Triage had been set up in the lobby and first floor of a hotel the Army had commandeered just inside the city limits of Santa María del Río. After Alfonso's minor scrapes and cuts had been attended to, he sought out Elena, who was pulling a jacket over her shoulders, presumably to mask her missing arm.

"How're you doing?" he asked.

"As well as possible, I guess. Physically fine, anyway. Did you check on Astrid?"

Alfonso shook his head. "No, not yet."

Marco spoke from the doorway behind him. "She's still in surgery, but the medics say she'll pull through."

"Thank God," Alfonso breathed. The relief in Elena's eyes was palpable.

"But she's clearly out of this fight. And so are the two of you."

Elena narrowed her eyes. "What do you mean?"

"The Americans are taking a more active role in the mission at the President's behest. They don't want you embedded anymore. Too dangerous, they say, and they're not wrong."

Elena shook her head incredulously. "Did you tell them our plan?"

"Acosta dismissed it right off. Not enough evidence. The scientific advisors in the US want them to try a few bombing strategies, conventional for now. There are rumors that the Americans have a working rail gun that they may be flying in. But no matter what, you're out."

Alfonso could see the same struggle he felt inside playing out on Elena's features. But she retained control of herself, gritting her teeth.

"And if we find proof?"

Marco shrugged weakly. "Then we'll talk. Right now, though, you need to rest, Elena. You're tough as nails, but this shit takes its toll."

Her eyes blazed. "I know its goddamn toll, Marco. Better than most."

"Yes, of course you do. So take some time. Attend to your needs." Addressing them both, he added, "Your things have been recovered and taken to your rooms, on the sixth floor."

He handed them keycards and began to leave. At the door, he turned back for a moment.

"We did all we could. You were both brilliant. No one can fault us. The fire wyrms just exceeded our reach."

#

The shower did Alfonso a world of good. Afternoon light slanted in through the glass doors of the balcony, illuminating sharply the contents of his backpack, now spread across the king-size bed.

As he saw it, three questions needed answering: Where is Amictlan? What exactly is Acuetzpalin? Where would it likely come ashore?

The strange hurricane spinning off shore might help answer the first. It had sprung up over the Sigsbee Abyssal Plain, the deepest point in the Gulf. If some gigantic opponent of fire wyrms existed in those waters, that would be a perfect home for it, a place it could escape detection by humans.

As for the identity of this erstwhile enemy, Alfonso was struggling. Rolling the desk chair to the side of the bed, he began picking through his books and notes.

The name Acuetzpalin, his web of expert friends had confirmed, didn't appear in any of the existing codices. But the description from the *Book of Forbidden Songs* had parallels in various sources. Colonial Yucatec dictionaries and the 16th-century *Relación de la Ciudad de Mérida* mentioned Itzam Cab Ain, a massive reptilian demigod connected with catastrophic floods. The word "itzam" meant whale in modern Yucatec Maya, which was a tantalizing clue. The root "itz" meant water. It was probably also the source of the name of the god Itzamna: house of itzam.

"House of the whale?" Alfonso muttered out loud to himself. "House of the water reptile?"

He thought of images of Itzamna in the *Dresden Codex*, emerging from a bicephalic wyrm. He thought of the Olmec shark god, an image so arresting he had hung it prominently in his apartment. He thought of Copan's Altar T, on which a strange aquatic reptile bore the tail of a fish, a motif found in quite a bit of Classical Maya iconography.

"Ah, damn. So many hints from the Yucatan Peninsula. I sure as shit hope we don't have to pied-piper these bastards all the way down to the Bay of Campeche."

Checking his email, Alfonso found that a colleague from Belize had sent an image of a mural from the ruins of Santa Rita Corozal. An immense sea creature stretched from edge to edge, covered with scales and edged with wave-like curls that suggested tentacles. Clambering over its hide were various organisms, and Alfonso recalled the epithet of Acuetzpalin: mother of water dogs.

Remembering that the *Florentine Codex* contained a description of that creature—known in Nahuatl as ahuizotl—Alfonso grabbed his copy of book eleven and hunted up the page. Roughly dog-like, the creature was said to have hands like a monkey, including one at the end of its tail. It dragged its prey to the depths of the sea—*in ahuehcatlan cahxitia*. The phrasing was suggestive of *amictlan*, which literally meant "watery place of the dead."

More hints waited in his inbox. The most tantalizing was a line from the Codex Chimalpopoca: *oncan hualquīzaya hualmonextiaya in atlan in motocayotia Acpaxapoh hueyi coatl ihuan in ixayac cihuatl auh in itzon huel quinehuihuilia in cihuah intzon.*

"And there would emerge," Alfonso translated aloud, using an app on his phone to record his voice for future reference, "appearing from the water, one called Acpaxapoh, a great serpent with a woman's face, with tresses of tendrils that truly resembled women's long hair."

Too much data from too many sources. Tantalizing, but not quite taking shape.

Standing, he pulled a shirt on. He needed to distract himself for a bit, allow the bits and pieces to rearrange themselves in his unconsciousness.

Opening the door, he walked across the hallway and knocked on Elena's door.

After a few seconds, she opened and gave a half smile. She was wearing a white terrycloth bathrobe, her light brown hair darkened by its dampness. In her hand was a glass of mescal, its pungent odor so evocative of earlier, happier times in Alfonso's life.

"Come on in," she said. "I was just watching the devastation and drowning my frustration with drink."

The television was on, the sound low. Images of both Sipakna and Xochitonal were split-screened as a commentator discussed their progress through the outlying suburbs of San Luís Potosí. Both had left smoking scars of destruction in their wakes. Alfonso knew he should feel renewed outrage and awe, but his heart was numb after all he had seen that day already.

"Want some Sacrificio?"

It took him a moment to realize she was referring to a brand of mescal.

"Hell, yes. Please."

She poured him a couple of fingers and gestured at the sofa. They sat down and sipped at their liquor, staring at the images of

American planes and tanks that pushed uselessly back at the fire wyrms.

"Shit," Alfonso said. "Have you talked to the technicians again? Even without Marco, we need to get that cannon and lure those freaking things out of the city."

"He's reassigned them, Alfonso. He knows me too well. Should've never told him anything. Sorry. I know it sucks."

As Sipakna batted a helicopter out of the air, sending it exploding into a school, Alfonso muttered a shaky curse. Elena knocked back her drink in a single gulp and stood to grab the bottle.

"But it's out of our hands, Alfonso. Isn't the Fifth Age supposed to end in a massive earthquake that destroys the world? Maybe the myths are true after all. Maybe our extinction is at hand. Maybe we deserve it."

Unstopping the bottle, she lifted it to her lips. Alfonso set his glass down and approached her slowly, putting a hand on her arm. With gentle movements, he took the bottle, set it down on the bar, and pulled her to him. She stiffened at his touch, not responding as he enfolded her in his arms. But as he continued to embrace her, she relaxed against him, crying softly.

Not hushing her, knowing by instinct how wrong that would be, Alfonso turned his face toward hers and pressed his lips against her trembling mouth. At first, she simply let him kiss her, but then something quickened in her, and she returned that kiss with eager hunger, burning breath and questing tongue.

Alfonso's right hand plunged into her damp hair as his mouth dropped to her neck, to the hollow of her shoulder. She gave a quiet moan, and he pulled on the sash of her robe, sliding his hand down her sternum, between her breasts. Easing the terrycloth open, he started to slip it from her shoulders.

Elena, gasping, pulled back. The pale skin that showed through the gap in her robe was flushed with excitement and shame.

"No. I don't want you to see…"

Alfonso pulled his shirt off over his head, revealing scars and strange tattoos. Then he pulled her close again, pressing his flesh against hers.

"I want you, Elena," he muttered, hoarse with need. "As you are."

Kissing her neck, he bent his head to her breasts, freeing them from the robe, licking in spirals. In a single, smooth motion, he slipped the robe from her shoulders, placing his hand on both her biceps.

Lifting his head, he looked at her, naked and trembling. Without a bit of irony or pity, his fingers grazed the pale blonde fuzz on the stump of her left arm.

"This makes you even more beautiful to me."

A dam broke in her, and she began to weep, seizing the back of his head and pressing her convulsing mouth to his, a kiss of salt and mescal and relief.

Then she drew him onto the bed, and they learned each other's bodies, broken and scarred and lovely both.

#

Afterward, spent and aglow, they lay there in the late afternoon light that was already edging toward evening, the sun low and bloody on the horizon.

"So tell me about these tattoos, Dr. Becerra," Elena said, turning on her side and running her hand over his abdomen.

"Well, this one over my heart is the glyph for my day sign: 1 Jaguar. That's what ritual day it was on the Aztec calendar when I was born on July 16, 1980. My right bicep has the *wacah chan* or World Tree, representing the union of earth with heaven and the underworld. It's a caiman, you see, upright, piercing the three worlds. The god of creation is a bird at the tip of its tail, amid flowers that blossom there in the highest heaven."

"And that was Tonantzin on your back, right? The Great Goddess?"

"Yeah. She's—I know this will strike you as silly, given your beliefs, but—she's my patron, you might say."

Elena leaned over and kissed the jaguar glyph, nipping lightly at his chest. "No, Alfonso, I don't think it's silly. She's sacred to you. I respect that. Now, what about these scars? No offense, but you don't seem like the street-fighting kind of guy."

Alfonso laughed. "Yeah, no. But I am the sort of moron who goes to Guatemala and pisses off a group of *mareros* because they're disrespecting Maya ruins. That, uh, did not end well for me. Spent several weeks in the hospital, in fact. They carved me up like a Christmas ham, those little bastards."

With a glint in her eye, Elena growled, "Well, at least they left some choice slices."

Running her tongue along the twisting vine of the scar that crossed his abdomen, she slipped her hand beneath the sheet …

… and her cell phone began ringing to the tone of Bob Dylan's "To Ramona."

"Ah, shit, I need to get this," Elena said, rolling over and grabbing her cell. "It's my assistant, Ramona Covarrubias."

She swiped the screen and hit speakerphone.

"Yeah, Ramona?"

"Oh, finally. I've been trying to track you down for two hours, and service sucks everywhere. Listen, there's this fisherman named Carlos Serrano who's been trying to get a hold of you all day. Sounded old on the phone. He told me that the Army ignores him, but that he's got something super important to show you. The signal kept dropping in and out, so I didn't catch it all. He kept saying 'water dogs,' though, and telling me there's help in the Gulf."

Alfonso sat up, eyes wide. "Where is he?"

"Sorry? Who's that?"

Elena rolled her eyes. "That's Dr. Becerra, Ramona."

"You mean the archeologist you …"

"Yes, Ramona," Elena cut in, mouthing the words *I'm sorry* to Alfonso with a crooked smile. "Now answer his question. Where is he?"

"As far as I know, he's almost there. He's driving to Santa María del Río to meet you."

CHAPTER FIFTEEN: MARCO

Eleven hours after the First Emergence, the estimated death toll had surpassed 100,000, a number Marco suspected was on the conservative side. Tens of thousands of wounded choked the halls of hospitals. Evacuation efforts had only been partially successful in the cities through which the fire wyrms had passed, and highways were clogged by accidents and breakdowns. Violence erupted amid the fleeing populations, horrible altercations with devastating consequences.

Separatist militia in the south had seized control of several cities; in the north, the cartels had done the same. Marco fielded multiple encrypted calls from generals in various military zones who were not at all pleased with the President's decision to embed American advisors in their headquarters. These critics of the commander-in-chief were about to get an even less pleasant surprise—

Russian and Chinese troops and planes had arrived in Mexico, and a now a US-led coalition was managing the crisis. Ron Acosta and his team had flown to Region IV HQ in Monterrey, Nuevo León, and were coordinating efforts in Zone 12—the city of San Luís Potosí—where even now the two fire wyrms struggled to rendezvous at the heart of the historical district.

Marco and his aides had remoted in to the regional headquarters from their mobile command post, but the President had essentially sidelined the team.

"The situation has evolved," the commander-in-chief had told him just moments ago. "I need you to secure all the remaining materiel, General, especially the ELF cannon, and to oversee the clean-up in Santa María del Río. I understand that some rogue chimaltontli are still in the area. Mop them up ASAP."

But right now, everyone's eyes were on the devastation in the state's capital. Sipakna had smashed through the towering Muñiz Werge building with idle rage, had tossed planes around at the airport like a massive and petulant child. Xochitonal had ripped the 100-meter tall antenna from the EME Building and used it as a spear to stab at passing helicopters and planes.

At present, both were trampling colonial edifices, kicking through cathedrals and museums at the heart of the city. All aircraft had been called back beyond a safe perimeter.

The Americans were about to try their ground-based laser.

The idea was—Acosta had explained—to direct a focused 150-kilowatt beam at the head of one of the fire wyrms. Simulations run by the US scientific advisors suggest that the beam would burn between overlapping chimaltontli and fry the monster's brain.

Watching the confrontation through multiple screens, Marco wasn't so sure.

A cordon of soldiers and trucks with surface-to-air missiles guarded the laser, which had been set up in the plaza fronting the ornate palace that housed the city's government.

Sipakna was bearing down on the armed forces there, her blue chitin stained purple by the light of the setting sun.

"Commence attack," Acosta called in English from with regional headquarters.

The laser was activated. Though mostly invisible, glimmering hints of it showed amid the sandstone dust that permeated the air in that warzone.

Drone cameras zoomed in on the fire wyrm's head, where the chitin in one spot had begun to glow cherry red. Sipakna jerked its torso down, but the laser tracked the movement easily. It began to bellow wordlessly into the ground, sending shockwaves along the paving stones.

Anticipation crawled in Marco's belly. He gripped the edge of the console where he stood. His aides held their breath.

"Look out!" someone called at HQ. "The other one is approaching fast!"

One of the screens filled up with the running form of Xochitonal. The protective cordon exploded into a hail of missiles and gunfire, but the green behemoth kept coming.

In its claws it still carried the 100-meter antenna it had wrested from the EME Building.

Leaping into the air as it had done before, it sailed over the truck on which the laser was mounted. With a horrifying roar, it twisted at the apex of its leap and slammed the antenna into the truck, killing the laser with a violent burst of sparks.

Landing atop the government palace, Xochitonal began laying waste in earnest, bashing men and trucks with hands and tail, vomiting corrosive bile over the entire plaza, which burst into flame and reduced the operation to slag in a question of seconds.

Then, in the gloaming of twilight, the two fire wyrms finally came together. Grappling, their claws interlocking, Sipakna's inner jaw emerged and clamped down on Xochitonal's throat, on which chimaltontli retreated momentarily to allow access to the actual flesh of the creature before reassembling around them, sealing the creatures together. Their tails wound round each other as well, with the mouth-like organs at each end between the pincer-digits osculating against each other, locked tight in an interlaced grip.

"Ah, goddamn us all to hell," Acosta spat. "They're mating."

#

The next ten minutes sped by in a series of top-level conversations, not all of which Marco was privy to.

Finally, the President contacted him on a secure line.

"General Navarro, I've made the call. Once the fire wyrms … uncouple, he coalition is going to herd them north into an uninhabited area—either in the mountains or below in the Wirikuta Desert—and then the US is going to launch an ICBM armed with a nuclear warhead. We can't afford to wait any longer. Nothing else has worked."

"With all due respect, Mr. President, there is still the alternate plan suggested by my science team …"

"No, I'm afraid we're not going to risk luring these bastards over 400 kilometers of populated areas on the off-chance that another monster will emerge from the sea to destroy them. Wrap up your duties there, Marco. Then get on a plane and go home. Be with your wife and daughters. I'm sidelining you. You did what you could, but now you're off the field. Am I clear?"

"Yes, sir, Mr. President."

After the connection ended, the general stood looking at the blank screen, considering the repercussions. Fallout, yes, but perhaps new emergences due to the detonation and the shockwaves it would set off.

He shuddered at the thought that this might just be the beginning, an overture to Armageddon.

Pulling his cell phone from a pocket, he noticed a missed call that he hadn't heard during all the chaos of the laser attack. It was Elena.

Selecting her name, he returned the call.

"Marco?" she said breathlessly, answering at the first ring.

"Yes, it's me." Defeat weighed heavy in his voice as he caught her up on the situation. "We couldn't stop them, El. So now the Americans, Russians, and Chinese have all convinced the President to use a nuclear weapon on Mexican soil."

"Wait, right in the middle of the city?"

"No. They'll wait till they're through … mating or whatever, and then they'll drive them north to a relatively unpopulated area."

"Okay, that means we still have time."

"Time for what? Elena, I've been pulled off the mission. I'm going home."

"Damn it, no, Marco. Wait. You wanted evidence, right? Something solid so that you would support our plan."

Marco closed his eyes and rubbed at his temples. "El, seriously, it's a little—"

"We've got your evidence, General. An eyewitness who saw Acuetzpalin in the 1930s. He's got documentary proof as well."

Unbidden, hope surged in Marco's chest.

"Wait, are you serious?"

"Yes. But we need your help. You've got to help us steal the ELF cannon and get it to the coast so we can lure them to their deaths."

That imperious tone transported Marco three decades into the past. He could almost feel her lips against his ear as he carried her, mostly skin and bones, a scrawny child mutilated and overcome with shock. Still, she whispered those words with deadly determination, her core will untouched by the kidnappers: "*Kill him.*"

Then Marco pointed his pistol without hesitation and put a bullet through that criminal's brain.

If he had obeyed Elena at six years of age, how could he refuse her now? She was unassailable in her command of him.

"Okay, shit … we'll do it. But where do we lure them? You keep saying to the coast, but where exactly?"

Elena cleared her throat. "Meet us at the hotel. Astrid's room. We'll explain everything to you."

CHAPTER SIXTEEN: CHARLOTTE

August 22, 1938—

This morning, we arrived at the coordinates the shrimper gave us. No sign of the monster. Chum on the waves, but they roil so hard that it is soon carried far off. We continue to look. They've cast the nets into to the see, trying to tempt it toward us.

Ah, but the unearthly bitch stays deep, nameless, inscrutable. Remorseless queen, hidden, cozening.

August 23, 1938—
Dark clouds have been building on the horizon all morning. The ship is pushing against headwinds as we ply deeper waters. Captain wants to return, says it's madness to continue. I've promised him more than I should. Pointed out what my husband does for a living, what he'll be willing to pay upon our return. There was doubt in his face, but he nodded at last.

"Two days. That's all I can give you, Mrs. Sewell. Then we'll be forced to return. Fuel will run out if not."

Forty-eight hours. If I come back empty-handed, what awaits me? James has moved from disapproval and worry to absolute rage at this point. The expedition has surely returned to port. The rodeo, in fact, is nearly finished. They will whisper my name, laughing and shaking their heads.

Madwoman.

Yankee.

Will they speculate as to my fidelity? Have folks concocted tales of hysterical passion for the salt-hardened captain? Ah, to hell with them all. How could I have not tried? What sort of woman would I be if I hadn't pursued the goddess when she reared her scaly head from the deep?

Shakespeare put it best:

> There is a tide in the affairs of men.
> Which, taken at the flood, leads on to fortune;
> Omitted, all the voyage of their life
> Is bound in shallows and in miseries.
> On such a full sea are we now afloat,
> And we must take the current when it serves,
> Or lose our ventures.

August 24, 1938—

By afternoon, I was convinced that all this effort would prove to be in vain, mocked by the smiling sky, the unsounded sea, the black smear on the horizon before us.

Then a white form twice the length of the boat streamed through the water to starboard. I caught a glimpse of fins, of probable lampreys in symbiotic kiss.

"It's here!" I shouted, turning to Carlos, who stood beside me. "Forty feet long, just like you said!"

Carlos shook his head. "No, señora. Not that. Big shark, not monster. Y no son cuarenta pies. Cuarenta metros. Forty yards."

I swung my eyes back to the water. A white whale shark broke the surface, skimming the chum.

Forty yards. What behemoth incarnation of unassailable nature have I been pursuing? What demoniac obsession drives me? Madness maddened, trebled in cataclysmic power. I'm leading these men and boys to their dooms. We should turn back immediately.

And yet. Just one more day. I ache to see her, even if her capture is impossible.

August 25, 1938—

The sea is calm at last, but my heart still trembles in crazy spasms and my soul gutters like an existential flame in the gale of terrible truth.

Midmorning. Sky dark like a bruise. Captain Maldonado called me to his cabin, pointed out our location on the charts. We were in the very depths, right over Sigsbee Deep.

"If we founder here," he snapped, "they'll never find us. We need to turn back now. That is a hurricane bearing down on us, ma'am. We can outrun it if we leave at once. And that's what we're going to do."

Defeated, I made a weak wave with my hand and returned to my spot at the gunwale. Perhaps the cyclonic winds would drive her to us during the return. There was still hope. I clung to it feverishly.

Then, as we fled, the hurricane gained unaccountable speed— pursuing us, it seemed, enraged at our flight. It struck with unbridled ferocity, the wind howling on and on, the sea leaping to spill in foamy flood upon the deck. As the swells built higher and higher, the ship groaned and dove from crest to trough, then climbed the next looming hill to begin another dive into the blackness of the sea and the night.

I knew I must leave the prow or be spilled into the sea. Seizing the railing, I began to make my unsteady way back in order to descend to my cabin.

Gonzalo was blocking my way, a feral grin on his face as he stood steady upon the heaving deck as if at finally at home in the heart of the maelstrom.

Seizing me, he hurled me down and straddled me, pinning my arms above my head with one arm as he unsheathed my knife with the other and used it to slice my blouse open. Buttons were snatched by the wind and waves, pelting against the bridge like projectiles from a gun.

I struggled with all my might as the bastard slid his hands under my brassiere and savagely fondled my breasts. I had not come all this way just to be raped by some twisted fisherman. I screamed and kicked, strove to bite his tattooed arms. He just laughed and dropped a hand to his pants.

At that moment, dozens of strange bioluminescent beings came clambering over the gunwales. The size of ponies, they sniffed at the wet and wild air with faces akin to savage, hairless dogs. From their slick, earless heads streamed strange dancing spikes of sparking blue, like crowns of St. Elmo's fire.

Each of their limbs ended in broad simian hands, webbed and agile. So did their powerful tails, I realized with shock, as one of the creatures whipped that fifth hand toward Gonzalo and wrapped its digits 'round his bastard neck, hauling him to his feet and choking him to death before me.

Dazed, I nonetheless managed to get to my feet and stumble aft. Carlos stood there near the stern, surrounded by a handful of the sea steeds as if Neptune himself had sent a herd to whisk the boy away.

"Miss Charlotte!" Carlos cried without fear, with childish joy beaming in his eyes despite the suck and surge of the sea, despite the monsters all around us. "They're *piko*! Water dogs!"

"What?"

"From the old stories. They help the goddess!"

And then, with a rushing roar like some mad typhoon, a horrifying cyclopean form burst from the sea, rising higher and higher above the ship. A spiraling Charybdis of waves slammed against the seiner, spinning it like a top. I clung to the gunwale and gaped in shock. Sickly green, groping at the streaming rain and spray with what seemed branches or tentacles, the massive leviathan appeared to hover for a moment, looming like some twisted antediluvian god, neither plant nor animal but something vastly more ancient.

Enormous eyes peered down at me, set high on that titanic form above a gaping and massive cephalopod beak from which a cacophonic cry burst forth, cracking the heavens and nearly sundering my heart.

Then, as her attendant water dogs howled in eldritch response and leapt into her tentacled arms, that ancient goddess fell back into the water, creating a tsunami that nearly capsized our ship, sending it rushing westward at breakneck speeds.

Now the storm has turned away from us. The sky is cloudless, full of myriad stars that are reflected in the surface of a sea that rolls placid and unknowable as it has for thousands of years.

Some will say I have failed. I will be mocked. No one will believe my tale, should I ever choose to recount it.

But—ah—I shall forever remember this night and count myself blessed.

For I once looked into the face of a goddess, and she did not destroy me.

CHAPTER SEVENTEEN: ELENA

"For I once looked into the face of a goddess, and she did not destroy me."

Elena closed the journal and repeated the line in Spanish. She couldn't help but cast a glance at Alfonso, whose back bore a noble image of an Aztec goddess that Elena's fingers and lips had caressed just an hour ago. The irony was striking, given how cruel and dismissive she had been to his unconventional beliefs on national television.

Astrid sat up straighter in her bed, eyes bright with tears. Marco fidgeted with the doorknob, making sure no one could walk in on their conversation.

Alfonso turned to Carlos Serrano, the weathered fisherman, a boy now grown old though not bent by those years, still hardy and hale like many elderly men of the coast.

"What happened to her afterward?"

"When the seiner limped back into port, Charlotte Sewell disembarked without a word and went straight home. I didn't see her for nearly a year. Nobody on board that boat told a soul what we'd seen. It was crazy and holy and just ... unbelievable. We went back to the work that put bread on our tables. We got our wages for her wild expedition, so I guess she paid Captain Maldonado after all.

"Then, the following summer, right after she lost the '39 fishing rodeo, Mrs. Sewell came 'round looking for me. Like a lot of others, I had moved on from the *Doña Angélica*, but that gringa tracked me down all the same. Said she and her husband were moving to Dallas, far from the Gulf. I got the feeling she wanted

128

to forget or to escape the temptation to go out there again, looking for the mother of piko. At any rate, she handed me the journal. 'I can't bring myself to destroy it,' she told me, 'but I also can't have it around any longer. It's yours, Carlos. Do what you want with it.' Something told me I should keep it. And so I have, for nearly eighty years."

Elena hefted the cracked leather. "Thank goodness you did."

"When that monster crawled out of the volcano, I knew our only hope was the goddess. The old stories say she's our protector. I tried calling, but everyone ignored me. I finally tracked down contact information for you, Dr. Baz, as I was driving toward all the devastation, determined to talk to somebody in charge. Miss Ramona told me right where you were, though the soldiers weren't going to let me through until you and Dr. Becerra showed up to escort me."

Elena glanced meaningfully at Marco. "So now you have it, General. Proof of Alfonso's theory."

"That this leviathan is the same as the Maya sea lizard or Olmec shark monster, also mentioned in the *Book of Forbidden Songs* as the enemy of the Lords of the Earth, dwelling in Amictlan, which is the Sigsbee Deep," Marco half-recited. "Do I have that right? Good. Now where did this thing come from? How do we know we can trust it to destroy the fire wyrms?"

Tapping the cast on her leg thoughtfully, Astrid spoke up.

"My initial hypothesis is that, given the periodic emergence of the fire wyrms, the Earth has evolved a response to that alien plague."

Alfonso jumped in. "And her appearance might be triggered by certain scale earthquakes. Back in July of 1937, around when Sewell's diary suggests sightings of Acuetzpalin started, there was a serious earthquake near Orizaba. It could have signaled a possible eruption, the first since 1845. Maybe the threat of an emergence awakened the, uh, *mother of water dogs* so that she could patrol the coast. Other elements of the journal check out, I should add. Storm Seven of that hurricane season developed in the Bay of Campeche and eventually curved northeastward through the Gulf of Mexico to expire weakly in Florida."

"Well, right now," the general said, "the hurricane spinning in the Gulf is spitting out weird energy signatures that seem to indicate it's moving toward the coast. But we don't have a clue as to its destination. And though you assured me you knew, none of you has said *where* exactly we're supposed to lure the fire wyrms."

Carlos laughed. "It's obvious if you speak Huasteca, sir. She's the 'mother of water dogs.' *Piko*, in our tongue. She'll come to the 'place of water dogs': *Tam Piko*. The city of Tampico."

Marco gave Elena a pregnant glance. It was time for Carlos to go so they could discuss the details of their highly illegal plan. But just hurrying the old man out was not an option. They needed his silence. They needed to respect what he had done, the effort he had made.

"Mr. Serrano, the risks you took to bring us this journal deserve public recognition. What would you say to being featured on the next episode of *Muñecos Cósmicos*?"

Twisting his cap in his gnarled hands, Carlos beamed in delight. "Ma'am, that would be a real honor."

"Tell you what I'm going to do. I'm going to have the network fly you down to Mexico City later this evening, once you've had a chance to rest in one of the rooms here in the hotel. My assistant Ramona, the one you spoke to on the phone, will pick you up in a company limousine at the airport—General Navarro, a flight can be arranged, can't it? Despite the closures?"

Marco caught on immediately. "Yes, Dr. Baz. I'll have one of my aides clear a runway for a network plane."

"Good. And then, Mr. Serrano, we'll put you up in a nice hotel for a few days, show you the sights, and by the end of the week, you and I will sit down for a nice casual interview that'll be part of the next episode. Sound good?"

"Sounds wonderful. Of course, I know you also need to keep me out of the way for a while—I'm no fool—but I'll take you up on the offer."

While Elena called up Ramona and made the arrangements, Marco had a guard find a suitable room for Carlos to freshen up and rest in.

"Good-bye for now, everyone," the elderly fisherman said as the guard came to escort him. "Best of luck with those *piko*. They are devilish fiends, very faithful to their mother."

After he had left, Marco got down to business.

"Okay, then. We lure them to Tampico. Elena, you said you could tweak the ELF cannon's programming to imitate their calls. Give me more detail."

"So the basic idea is to move the cannon close to coast first, about a hundred kilometers west of Tampico. The transport time will mask the operation and allow me to finish coding a routine that replicates the frequencies and durations of the vocalizations used by the fire wyrms to call each other over great distances. I fire that into the ground periodically with the same intensity they employed. In theory, they'll come toward the signal."

Marco rubbed his temple. "And so will coalition forces."

"By that time," Alfonso said, "we're betting cloud cover from the hurricane will make it harder for anyone to stop us. But you'll have to do the rest. You'll have to convince the President that we've come too far at that point."

"Easier said than done. Of course, I haven't been wasting time. They sidelined me and a bunch of other high-ranking officers when they brought the Americans, Russians, and Chinese on board. These are men and women whose confidence in the President frayed long ago, with his mishandling of other crises. And, of course, no one wants a nuclear detonation in Mexico. I'm pretty certain I can drum up the support we need. Once the ... Mother emerges from the storm, the ball will be completely in our court. Now tell me—how exactly are you going to do that?"

Astrid shrugged. "The presence of the fire wyrms should be enough to get her to attack them. Put two natural enemies face to face, and that's usually enough."

Alfonso pulled his phone from his jacket pocket. "But I've got a back-up. If I have to, I'll prompt her using a hymn from the *Book of Forbidden Songs*. 'Innan in Ahuitzomeh.' Means 'Mother of Water Dogs.' Here, listen."

The archeologist played a snippet of an old man singing in Nahuatl. Elena felt a wave of admiration for him that went beyond her physical desire and her growing emotional attachment—

Alfonso had insisted on pursuing a line of investigation that only he fully believed in, and despite lack of support from nearly everyone, he had found an answer to their crisis. Yet he never lorded it over them. He was not smug at all. He deferred to the expertise of his other team members and had readily admitted just a few hours ago beneath the rubble that his plan was nothing without Elena's knowledge, research, and skill.

So she was careful now in addressing the problem she saw.

"Alfonso, my only concern is … how would Acuetzpalin know Nahuatl?"

"Ah, yes, great question, El."

Marco's eyebrow went up at the easy exchange and the archeologist's use of that nickname. Alfonso didn't appear to notice: he fiddled with the recording app for a second or two.

"Okay, so there are also a bunch of nonsense words at the end that might be the real, uh, summoning spell."

He played a string of syllables that might as well have been Nahuatl, too, for all Elena understood. But something else tickled the back of her mind, bugging her.

"Not sure how, exactly, but I think those are important. Let it roll around in my subconscious for a while. I'll figure it out."

Marco put his hand on the doorknob.

"All right. Under the pretense of returning it to Mexico City, I'm going to have the cannon loaded into a sling and a helicopter assign to transporting it. I'll need another thirty minutes or so to make calls and get a path cleared for us. If I can convince enough of my allies, we might be able to create satellite blind spots and have a pretty solid shield of soldiers and weapons. God forbid we have to get into a fight with coalition forces, but I want to be ready just in case.

"We might all end up in prison together, but Elena and Dr. Becerra, meet me at the command module in half an hour."

Astrid cleared her throat. "Uh, aren't you forgetting someone?"

Elena shook her head. In her mind's eye, she saw the young biologist, wounded on the ground, covered in Roberto's blood, screaming.

"You need to recover, Astrid."

"Ah, no. Don't make me pull rank on you, Elena."

Alfonso laughed.

"She's got you there, El."

Marco's face clouded over with puzzlement.

"What do you mean?"

Elena smiled despite herself. "The little bitch is a Nobel nominee. Only one in the room. She's a superstar in the scientific community. Wields privilege. Doesn't care that she'll be a burden."

"Whatever, Ms. I-host-the-most-popular-science-show-in-Mexico. You're going to be transporting a two-ton ELF cannon three hundred kilometers. You can manage a scrawny woman with a cast on her leg."

"We'll take you," Marco said, cutting off the banter. "Get her ready and roll her over to the command center in thirty minutes. With luck, the operation will be good to go by then."

He unlocked the door and left.

"Okay, guys," Astrid said, giving a conspiratorial wink. "Out with it. You hooked up, didn't you?"

Elena could feel herself blushing. "You're certainly nosey for a certified genius."

Alfonso's face lit up with a ridiculous grin that Elena nonetheless found endearing.

"Oh, shit, it is that obvious?"

"Uh, yeah. The pheromones in this room alone are enough to drive wild baboons into a frenzy. I'm surprised Marco didn't notice, Elena. You're like a fourth daughter to him. Thought he'd be more overprotective."

Elena thought of his constant deference to her. "Not likely. He knows he'd catch hell if he tried to micromanage my personal life."

"Well, perhaps you can control his possible overreaction to my back-up protection plan." Astrid gestured at the laptop on her lap. "While the two of you were doing the nasty, I was coordinating with Roberto and Silvia's web of experts. I'm pretty sure I have a way to keep the coalition off our tail.

"We make them believe a shitload of fire wyrms are about to emerge."

#

Twenty minutes later, Elena shouldered her pack and met Alfonso in the hall. He gave her a quick but determined kiss on the lips.

"You ready for this?"

The consequences of the mission had been stewing inside her for some time, but she felt she had made peace with the probable end of her career.

"No, but that's never stopped me before. Sometimes you just have to act. Can't think about what happens next. Do what must be done at that second."

He curled his fingers around hers briefly as they waited for the elevator. His touch was ridiculously electric. Who could have predicted it? The man she had thought she despised clicked perfectly in all the ways that counted.

The rest she didn't give a shit about, anyway.

"No matter what happens next, El, I don't regret … us. Not a single conflicted moment."

"Ditto."

A guard had already brought a wheelchair to Astrid's room, so then it was just a matter of easing her slight form into it and heading out the hotel doors to the command module at the far end of the parking lot. Marco, two colonels, and a half-dozen aides emerged immediately.

"We're set," the general told them, waving them toward the street, where a Chinook Mexico had acquired from Argentina was being hooked up via a cable to the ELF cannon.

Elena leaned closer to him as the rotors started spinning.

"You got the support we need?"

"That and more. I had to talk some of them off the ledge. They'd stage a freaking coup at this point, they're so pissed off."

"Hrm. Maybe you can use that as leverage later. Tell the President you saved his ass."

Marco smiled. "If we make it, El. If we make it. We're putting ourselves right smack dab in the middle of this crisis, trapping ourselves between monsters of the deep and fire wyrms, between a coalition of the most powerful militaries on the planet and the will of my commander-in-chief. I'm afraid it's going to get really tough for me to keep my promise today."

Taking his arm, she drew him up short while the others walked ahead.

"Marco, you've done more for me than anyone, ever. You don't owe me a damn thing anymore, okay? Consider yourself absolved from the promise. We've got to think about the country, not each other."

Tears stood out in his eyes as he nodded.

"Okay, sweetie. Whatever you say."

Shaking her head with exasperation, she hugged him briefly before they both resumed their march toward destiny.

CHAPTER EIGHTEEN: ALFONSO

Alfonso had been holding back his furious indignation for far too long already, but he waited until Marco, Elena, and Astrid were deeply involved in their several tasks before getting started. He didn't want them asking too many questions. The fallout from this mission was going to be ugly for everyone, but the archeologist knew that people might die once he acted. He would shoulder that blame alone.

The coalition intended to nuke the fire wyrms in the Wirikuta Desert, an ancestral holy land of the Huichol people. Alfonso himself had spent a week out upon that stony sand with a shaman, ingesting peyote and knitting himself more deeply into the fabric of the cosmos through the traditional rites of the Huichol. That indigenous nation deserved to know of the coming desecration. Its elders needed the opportunity to act in defense of their cultural patrimony. Their allies in various academic fields must advocate for their tribal sovereignty.

Plus, the resulting chaos of the leak would keep the military even more off-balance and further facilitate the team's summoning of Acuetzpalin.

So, as the helicopter bore them and the cannon over the mountains and toward the Gulf coast, Alfonso began to compose an email, blind carbon-copying every journalist and blogger he knew, that revealed the coalition's plan and the President's refusal to attempt his science advisors' alternate proposal. Hoping to appeal to the religious sensibilities of the Huichol, he closed the message by mentioning their water goddess, Nacawé, and how her serpents would rise from the Gulf to destroy the alien beasts.

It only took five minutes for the first blog to post the text of his message, citing "a source high-up in the Mexican government."

Within fifteen minutes, the hashtags #savewirikuta and #nonukesinMX had begun to trend.

A half hour after Alfonso sent the message, Elena stopped her urgent exchanges with the cannon technicians and called to him, pointing at the laptop perched on her legs.

"This is you, isn't it?" she asked.

"What is?" he asked, trying to feign ignorance.

"Don't pretend you don't know what the hell I'm talking about, Alfonso. Look at the Televisa website."

There were several clips: leaders decrying the government, calling people to action; activists taking to the streets to protest beneath the street lamps; buses loading up with Huichol folk and their allies, heading out to the desert for a massive sit-in.

Talking heads ripped into the President, calling him "traitor" and "malinchista," saying that once again Mexico would be selling its northern territories to the USA.

In the midst of all of this, the fire wyrms had uncoupled and were rampaging through the rest of San Luís Potosí, moving steadily northward.

"Well," Alfonso finally said, "whoever leaked the plan is going to be in a shitload of trouble, huh?"

"Jesus, Al! Did you at least mask your identity a little? Use a fake email account or something?"

"I wasn't really thinking about what would happen next. I just … did what had to be done at that second."

Elena narrowed her eyes for a moment. Then, unexpectedly, she laughed. "Ah, hell. Serves me right for giving anyone advice. It was actually a brilliant move, even if your implementation was a little half-assed."

The compliment was good enough for him.

#

It took them a little over ninety minutes to reach a spot just east of Pánuco at the northernmost edge of Veracruz state. An army convoy was waiting for them, but Marco calmed everyone's jumpy nerves.

"Along with the governor of Tamaulipas and the mayor of Tampico, the generals in charge of the eighth and twenty-sixth military zones have thrown their support behind us," he explained. "They've put four regiments at my disposal, including the motorized cavalry you see outside and a couple of infantry battalions in route to ground zero, just south of Tampico."

The stars were invisible now as clouds streamed in from the Gulf. With the help of some of the soldiers, Alfonso got Astrid out of the helicopter while Marco went off to meet with the battalion leaders and Elena took her team to get the cannon ready.

Struggling against grass and rocks, he rolled Astrid to a stop right beside the control panel—there was no time to set up a platform like before.

Elena nodded at them.

"Guys, I'm going to have my hands full with this. Alfonso, keep tabs on the fire wyrms. Let Astrid know when it's time, okay?"

"You bet, El."

She turned and shouted a few commands at the technicians above the dull whistling of the wind.

The ELF cannon hummed to life.

"Alright," Elena said out loud. "Re-orienting to minus 45 degrees."

The sonic weapon tilted toward the ground.

"Feeding in mimetic sequence 01."

Her five fingers danced across the keyboard faster than Alfonso could type with both his hands and several cups of coffee in his veins. His heart ached with admiration.

"Programming five-minute loop."

The hum grew more intense, building toward release.

"Initiating sequence ... now!"

The ground beneath their feet began to thrum in strange, roiling waves. Audible sound bled around the edges of the beam, sending drabs of weird, wailing frequencies buzzing herky-jerky through the air.

Alfonso managed to wait for nearly the entire five-minute loop, but finally curiosity got the better of him. He pulled out his phone, peering at the live drone feed from San Luís Potosí.

Sipakna and Xochitonal had paused their rampage and were bending in curiosity, laying their taloned hands against the broken asphalt. Then, visibly agitated or excited, they howled wordlessly at the heavens before hurling their own subsonic cry at the earth below them.

"Elena, they're responding!"

"I know, I know. Hang on. I'm plugging in mimetic sequence 02, the response."

As she did so, the first sequence halted and the ground stilled for a moment. Then a tremor shook the area slightly, like an aftershock.

"Okay, here it goes. Initiating sequence 02!"

Arrhythmic vibrations stuttered beneath them, travelling through the bedrock at some seven kilometers per second.

Alfonso kept his eyes glued to his phone, waiting.

The fire wyrms crouched, waiting.

Then Sipakna pushed her inner jaw out into the steaming night and howled with what might have been rabid joy.

The Lords of the Earth turned east and began to run.

"Now!" Alfonso cried. "Do it now, Astrid!"

The biologist flashed a devilish smile and slapped her right index finger against her tablet.

All across Mexico, every volcanic observation instrument wailed reports of impending earthquakes and eruption.

With the help of Silvia's colleagues, Astrid had hacked CENAPRED and simulated mass emergence. It would take the government hours to investigate and disprove the false alarms.

#

Ten minutes later, the convoy was transporting the team and the cannon along dusty narrow roads near the Pánuco River. The coast lay about an hour away through sprawling ejidos and a patchwork of fields and forests, a landscape whose possible beauty was effaced by the rain that had begun to fall in thick sheets.

Inside the large transport assigned to them, Alfonso and the other two scientists kept a close eye on the news. Coalition forces were trying to stop Sipakna and Xochitonal, but the behemoths had already pushed past the bulk of those forces.

"I suspect," Astrid said, "just from stride measurements and other observational data we've acquired, that the fire wyrms could cover the four hundred kilometers or so separating them from us in two hours or so, if ..."

"If no one were trying to stop them," Elena continued. "Yeah, that's probably right. We've thinned out the Mexican Army quite a bit, but the goddamn Americans, I swear."

Her cell phone rang.

"Hang on, guys, it's Marco. Yes? Okay, just a moment."

She glanced at the phone and put the call on speaker.

"Everyone can hear you now, General."

"Alright. Interesting news. Distressing is perhaps a better word, though the situation ultimately benefits us. Between my alliance-building, Dr. Estrada's CENAPRED hack, and Dr. Becerra's unauthorized leak, confidence in the President has been completely undermined. Five minutes ago, a coup was carried out by eight of the twelve regional commanders. That military junta has temporarily suspended the constitution and declared martial law."

"Holy shit!" Alfonso hadn't expected this at all. He imagined none of them had.

"That was my reaction, too, Dr. Becerra. I've been contacted by the generals. They want to know what we need."

Elena gave a vicious nod. "Good. Tell them to get everyone the hell out of the way. No one should try to stop the fire wyrms. Let's get them here fast with as little collateral damage as we can manage."

Alfonso gave her a thumbs-up and leaned forward to add, "See if they can stop the coalition from interfering with us, too."

"Yes, though I'm sure they're working on that already. Okay, team, forty-five more minutes. We'll see how this all pans out."

#

The caravan moved inexorably forward against the wind, past the broad Pueblo Viejo Lagoon, pushing through curtains of rain as it hit Highway 180 and turned north toward Tampico Alto. The town had been evacuated earlier that day due to the looming hurricane, and now six hundred infantrymen had completely secured its streets to allow the convoy to transport the cannon through its heart and then down toward the Gulf itself.

The general had called them back with word that the military junta had in effect demanded that coalition forces halt all movements in Mexico. But neither the US nor Russia was particularly accepting of the situation, declaring the coup in contravention of multiple international treaties.

The American president had gone on TV to make some outlandish promises about what that government would do to protect its people.

As the vehicles rolled at last on to the wind-lashed sand, Astrid let out a sharp moan.

"Son of a bitch. What if they drop a bomb on us, guys?"

Elena and Alfonso exchanged a tense glance. He wanted nothing more than to pull her from the jeep, to press his mouth to hers there at the edge of the world, amid the crashing waves and driving rain. Then, if it all ended, he would at least taste the salty-sweet perfection of her lips one last time.

"Ah, shit, Astrid," Elena said. "We'll be immortalized. Probably get a posthumous Nobel. Keep your chin up, friend."

The convoy came to a stop on the emptiest stretch of sand. The sea and sky had merged into a swirl of inky black madness, winds howling over the dunes like harbingers of destruction.

From the heart of that dark storm came flickers of electric blue fire.

As weapons were ranged round, Elena and her technicians prepared the cannon. Alfonso sat with Astrid inside the jeep— there was no question of getting the biologist out, not when they might need to abandon the area in haste very soon. Together, they monitored the fire wyrms' movements as tracked by a drone with night vision. The pair of leviathans had just crossed the Pánuco River near Chajir Lagoon, sprinting with mad abandon from the highlands toward the coast. As they ran, they now twisted their mighty heads toward the earth, dragging their tails along the ground.

"They've heard the sequence," Astrid muttered. "Look at them redouble their speed. Holy hell, Alfonso."

"Stay here for a minute. Let me check with Elena about something. I'll be right back."

Astrid started to object, but then a smile dawned on her face. "Oh, I get you. A little smooch at the edge of cataclysm, huh? Go for it, Al."

"You're a weirdo, did anyone tell you that? Brilliant, too, but definitely weird."

She waggled her eyebrows. "Hey, I know mating rituals when I see them. Be safe. There are monsters out there."

Rolling his eyes, Alfonso dashed out into the lashing rain. Aided by the headlights of a half-dozen vehicles, soldiers were already reorienting the ELF cannon toward the sea.

Elena stood to one side, her hair almost black with damp, her blouse clinging to her skin in ways that made Alfonso's nerves sing. Marco waited beside her, his hands loose and ready at his sides as if at any moment he might draw his pistol and take on the storm itself to protect her.

"They're probably a half hour away," Alfonso called out as he approached. "By now, Acuetzpalin should have sensed them. We'll need to be ready to get the hell out of her way when she hits the beach."

The general wiped rain from his eyes. "I've already given the order. I was just telling Dr. Baz that we may have to leave the cannon behind, though."

"That's fine. I've got ideas for major refinements, anyway. If we don't go to prison, I'll spend a lot of time redesigning it."

"Hey, uh, El?" Alfonso touched her shoulder. "Can I talk to you?"

She glanced at the general. "Give us a moment, would you?"

Arching an eyebrow with restrained surprise, Marco walked a few paces away to give them privacy.

"What's up, Alfonso?"

He swallowed heavily, trying to get himself sorted.

"Look, whatever happens in the next few minutes, I wanted you to know that I'm glad we … got to know each other better. You're an amazing woman, and even if nothing more comes of this crisis, even if you're not interested in, you know, a relationship with me, I'm proud to have you as a friend and colleague. We—"

"Oh, shut up, Alfonso," Elena said, stepping closer and kissing him deeply. He pulled her against him for a couple of seconds, feeling her flesh quiver with the same coruscating flame that filled his veins. Then they pulled away, eyes glinting with desire.

Neither said a word. There was no need.

Around them, the wind had become a gale. Rain pelted their skin, stinging and constant. A spotlight hit the churning waves of the sea, roaming, searching.

The packed sand soon began to shudder with the rapid approach of the Lords of the Earth. Alfonso bent over his phone, saw that the fire wyrms had crossed a river some twenty kilometers to the east.

Any minute, the behemoth pair would be upon them.

So where was their enemy?

CHAPTER NINETEEN: MARCO

Marco scowled at the embrace, like a father who catches his teenage girl on the porch kissing her date goodnight. Alfonso Becerra was a good man, would treat Elena better than any of her former lovers had. Still, letting go was difficult. She had absolved him of his promise to never let her get hurt again, but the general doubted he would ever fully be free of the bleak bonds that tethered his heart to hers.

Battalion leaders reported to him periodically as they waited. Everyone was at the ready. The storm raged around them as the fire wyrms bore down on their location.

Sentries at the perimeter radioed in—the creatures had arrived.

"God damn it, Dr. Becerra," he growled, approaching the two scientists, who stood in the relative shelter and windbreak of the cannon. "Where is this goddess of yours? We're sitting ducks out here!"

"I don't know, General. Maybe she's waiting till they actually reach the beach."

"Do you mean I should let them start killing these men first? That's not acceptable!"

"Okay, okay. Of course it isn't." The archeologist turned to Elena. "Let's do it. You can jack my phone into the console, can't you?"

"Yes. Hang on."

At Marco's confused expression, Alfonso explained. "The hymn. That's why she pointed this thing at the sea. In case we needed to call Acuetzpalin ourselves. Luckily, we have the song recorded."

"Alright, Alfonso," Elena called, "bring me your cell."

The archeologist hurried over to the console. Marco followed close.

"Let me bring up the recording," Alfonso said as Elena reached out her hand.

As he lifted his phone, the prevailing winds shifted out of the north and a roaring gust ripped the device from his grip, sending it spinning off into the dark.

Without needing orders, the four soldiers guarding the cannon snapped into action, rushing after it, flashlights dancing across the sand.

To no avail. The phone had disappeared into the roiling sea, which even now surged closer and closer to the parked convoy.

"Of all the goddamn luck!" shouted Alfonso, clenching his hands into fists.

"Calm down," Elena said. "There's another option. I'll rig a mic up, and then you can sing it. You know the language; you have the skill to perform the hymn."

"Yeah, but I didn't freaking *memorize the words*, El! Especially not all the gibberish at the end."

Marco watched how calm she had gotten, her one hand twisting at cables that protruded from the back of the console, working quickly and without panic to jury-rig a solution to the technical issues. Caught between the monsters and the hurricane, she continued, undaunted.

"It doesn't matter, really, as long as you remember the rhythm. Don't you see? Short and long vowels. Nahuatl has sounds of different durations. It's a code, Alfonso! The words don't matter … the rhythm does."

Alfonso's expression went from horror to surprise and then to excitement all in the space of a few seconds.

"Oh, my God, Elena. You're freaking right! That's absolutely brilliant. The rhythm, the rhythm …"

The archeologist started humming to himself, drumming his fingers lightly on his chest and abdomen in strange, syncopated patterns.

Elena was stripping the wires of a pair of headphones and splicing them with uncanny nimbleness into the control panel.

After fiddling with a few dials and knobs, she tapped on one of the ear speakers and was rewarded by a corresponding wave of rumbling frequencies from the cannon.

"Here we go, Alfonso. We're using the same frequencies as the fire wyrms. Hold the earpiece to your mouth and sing." Her voice took on an intensity that not even the storm could match, a dark surety that had galvanized Marco into action thirty years before. Alfonso was transfixed. "You've got this, do you hear me? Your whole life has prepared you for this moment. Sing, baby. Call that goddess forth."

Alfonso grabbed the headset and began to chant, his rich baritone transformed into the eldritch wailing of some primordial deity. The alien rhythms cycled again and again, building in intensity.

They were answered, not by the sea, but by horrific roars from the dunes.

The fire wyrms had come to a halt two hundred meters away, lit up glimmering green and blue by spotlights and headlights, their reptilian heads hidden by the swirling clouds.

Xochitonal lowered himself into a crouch, spreading wide his outer jaw. His nightmare eyes blazed across the sand, glaring right at Elena.

Marco pulled his pistol by instinct, stepped in front of the physicist.

"No way, you goddamn bastard. You stay the hell away from her."

The fire wyrm dug its claws into the dunes. Sipakna crouched beside it, ready as well.

Alfonso's chant had reached an impossible climax, sending shudders of sound through air, rain, sand.

Then he fell silent.

"Everyone, get out of the way!" the archeologist shouted. "She's here!"

Grabbing Elena, Marco started sprinting toward the jeep where Astrid waited. Alfonso came hot on their heels.

As they ran, the general looked over his shoulder. Exploding from the waves came a flood of pale creatures, pounding the wet sand on all fours, haloes of electric blue streaming from their sleek heads, prehensile tales slapping a strange fifth hand against the ground as if to propel them forward even faster.

The ahuitzomeh. Piko. Water dogs.

The three of them reached the jeep and piled inside, Marco in the passenger seat, the scientists in back.

"And now the band's back together!" exclaimed Dr. Estrada. She was holding up her tablet, pointing it toward the beach ahead of them.

"What the hell, Astrid?" Alfonso cried.

"I'm live-streaming everything. Ten thousand viewers right now, friend. Like you said, the public has a right to know about … Holy shit, guys!"

They all stared forward in astonishment as the cataclysmic battle began.

The fire wyrms, roaring in rage at the approach of the water dogs, reared back and sprayed their corrosive acid over that first wave of attackers. Some of the mustang-sized creatures swerved out of the way with agile leaps, but many were engulfed in the flaming bile.

A second and third wave of water dogs came bursting from the sea as the survivors of the vanguard hurled themselves onto the fire wyrms, clambering up their uneven chitin. They filled the air with raucous sounds, midway between barks and the screech of eagles.

Xochitonal and Sipakna surged erect, trying to sweep their attacks away with those long, vicious talons, which managed to impale some water dogs or slice them open, spilling luminescent innards onto the dunes below.

But the fire wyrms were soon swarmed with hundreds of these aquatic monsters, and the attack began in earnest. The haloes of glowing blue engulfed the entire body of each water dog, and with their webbed, simian hands, they began to pry at the chimaltontli, stunning the chitin fragments with electrical shocks before pulling them free and hurling them to the sand. Some of the chimaltontli retained enough vitality to seize a water dog or two as they fell, yanking the attackers free of their mighty host. For the most part, however, the ahuitzomeh were managing to wrest large swatches of armor away.

Dr. Estrada gasped, turning the tablet around to face her. "Ladies and gentlemen, the water dogs are stripping away the fire wyrms' defenses! It's like they're setting things up for …"

Marco looked out the passenger window and saw the tsunami looming above the ravenous foam. Turning to the driver assigned to their jeep, the general shouted. "Retreat, Private! Put this thing in reverse and get us back, now!"

As they jolted backward along the strand, Marco lifted the radio and gave a general command. "Everyone, move as far away as you can! The Mother is on her way. Repeat, *the Mother is on her way!*"

The tidal wave struck the beach, tossing the ELF cannon aside, sweeping several vehicles toward the dunes. A wave of water came rushing at their jeep, and Marco gripped the door handle tightly as the three scientists behind him gasped in fear. Their driver floored the accelerator, but the water reached them all the same, lifting them from the beach and thrusting them at an angle toward the dunes.

They slammed into a palm tree and held fast as the surge rushed over the hood but got no higher.

"Look!" Dr. Becerra shouted. "It's Acuetzpalin!"

Xochitonal, flailing with frantic twists, had spat up another flood of flaming acid, and by its light, they could make out the beast that had arisen from the sea. Its long, almost whale-like body was partly in the sea, but its upper half—a torso fringed by long and powerful tentacles, a torpedo-shaped head with enormous eyes and a terrifying beak—filled the beach in front of the fire wyrms.

"Oh, wow!" Dr. Estrada exclaimed. "Those of you at home, take a look at those webbed forelimbs! They're mesaxonic and weight-bearing, like those of a prehistoric *Rodhocetus*! That means she can drag itself along on land, folks."

Acuetzpalin wasted no time. Tentacles whipped out and coiled around Xochitonal's legs. The sea monster hauled back, yanking the fire wyrm from its feet. As the behemoth fell, the water dogs swarmed to its torso, working in tandem to rip off as many chimaltontli as possible.

Xochitonal hit the ground with a teeth-rattling concussion. Acuetzpalin surged further onto the beach while simultaneously pulling her enemy closer.

Sipakna howled, moving to stop her, but the water dogs on Xochitonal leapt as one onto the blue-hued fire wyrm, clambering to its jaws and electrocuting the chimaltontli that pumped noxious gasses into its lungs.

Xochitonal was slashing at the tentacles around its legs. It managed to sever one, and Acuetzpalin gave a piercing shriek before lifting a half dozen of those appendages and slamming them into the exposed flesh of the fire wyrm.

Rancid ichor blossomed out into the slackening rain as Acuetzpalin dug her tentacles deep into her enemy's guts, pushing herself forward onto his body with her powerful forelimbs until her long, tapering tail and weaker hind limbs were completely out of the water.

She bent her beak to Xochitonal's neck and began to rip into that pale, alien meat.

"Oh, shit, Marco!"

Elena's hand gripped his shoulder and then pointed.

"The chimaltontli! They're reviving … attacking her!"

The red nerve tendrils slapped against Acuetzpalin's scaly skin, flinging the chitin fragments onto her body, where they attempted to latch on with their strange mouths like lampreys.

Marco knew they would have to help her.

"All infantrymen," he called over the radio, "advance on the Mother and engage the chimaltontli. Aim for their unarmored underbellies."

Squads of soldiers rushed toward the colossal creature and started sniping at her attackers. The wind had calmed even further, and the rain was tapering off to a drizzle. Spotlights fell on the titanic struggle just in time to illuminate Acuetzpalin's evisceration of Xochitonal—all her tentacles pulled out at the same time, dragging strange, bloated organs out in gouts of alien gore. As she drew back, she pulled her vicious beak down the fire wyrm's exposed belly, spilling the rest of its rank guts out upon the dunes.

Sipakna, who had finally managed to bat the water dogs off its face, looked down at its dying companion and howled with unholy fury. In two swift strides, it reached Acuetzpalin and wrapped its arms around her upper body, lifting her into the air and slamming her down against the beach.

Soldiers went flying into the waves or tumbling to the sand. Marco braced himself: sure enough, their jeep bounced violently, once.

"Ow! Titanic body slams, those of you viewing at home," Estrada quipped. "Not good from the bleachers at all, trust me."

As Sipakna raised a taloned fist, every last water dog on the beached swarmed the fire wyrm, sending discharges of electricity into its exposed flesh.

Acuetzpalin flung out tentacles, wrapping them around her enemy and pulling herself up from the sand till she clung to Sipakna's chest like a nursing infant. The fire wyrm tried to punch at the pointed head of its opponent, but the blows were hampered by the ineluctable squeezing of those powerful tendrils.

Sipakna's tail whipped again and again against the Mother's back, ripping ugly welts open down that scaly hide. In response, water dogs congregated at the base of the tail, concentrating their energy discharge till they had immobilized it.

The fire wyrm's exposed throat bubbled as if preparing to spew acid onto Acuetzpalin, but the mother simply sealed its jaws shut with her last free tentacle and kept squeezing.

Sipakna fell to its knees, flesh swelling horribly between the tightened spirals that constrained it.

Then that pale skin split like a melon in multiple place, spraying gore over the soldiers arrayed below, and the fire wyrm toppled backward into the calming sea.

Now in her own element, the mother loosened all but a few tentacles, giving a harsh, harrowing screech that called her children to her, bounding like terrifying puppies over the sand and into the waves. They began to glow as one, a bright scintillation of gaudy blue, lightning come alive in the very Gulf. Then a whirlpool began to eddy faster and faster around their mother, and with a vast sigh like the coo of an infant god, Acuetzpalin and her attendants disappeared from view, dragging the fire wyrm after them into the unsoundable depths.

Everyone sat silent for a moment, staring at the stilling sea.

No words could express their collective awe.

"Whoa!" Dr. Estrada shouted to her tablet, addressing the Internet. "That was something, wasn't it folks? And lucky me, the Mother left a gigantic alien corpse behind! Nobel Prize, here I come! Okay, battery's nearly dead. Time to go. This is Astrid Estrada, along with Alfonso Becerra, Elena Baz, General Marco Navarro, and Private … uh …"

"Ricardo Sanz, ma'am," the driver muttered with a grin.

"And Private Ricardo Sanz, signing off after saving the world. Goodnight, Mexico!"

As the moon shone down on Xochitonal—defeated at last by science and myth—relief made it easy for everyone to laugh.

Marco twisted around in his seat, hoping to see a rare smile light up Elena's face.

There it was, that elusive glint of gladness, erasing the sad shadows as she stared into Alfonso's eyes, taking his hands in hers.

Perhaps now, the general thought with a mix of joy and regret, *we can both put the past behind us.*

EPILOGUE: ZONGOLICA

Three months later, a rented car made its way up winding mountain roads to the town of Zongolica. It slowed as it entered the city limits, allowing its passengers to take in the sights, to study the patterns of its narrow streets, to greet the pedestrians that made their peaceful way to and from their colorful homes.

At last the car drew up to the entrance of the Becerra family abode, and three people got out, stretching and laughing.

Alfonso Becerra reached out and hugged his son Ramiro to him, tousling his hair.

"We're here, kid."

"Finally! The flight was fun, but this drive was crazy boring, Dad."

"Blame it on the person who just *had* to listen to a science podcast the whole way."

Elena Baz slammed the door shut and gave him the finger with her bionic hand, smiling sweetly. "I love you, too, dumb-ass. Alright, Ramiro. We can listen to music on the way back ... as long as you pick the songs and not your dad."

"Deal!"

As the three approached the house, hugging and tickling each other, Alfonso's mother stepped onto the porch and gave a shout of delight.

"Finally, you're here!" she said as she hugged Alfonso and Ramiro. Then she turned to the physicist, peering up at her green eyes. "You're Elena, aren't you? Victoria Becerra, enchanted. We love your show, dear."

"Thanks, Doña Victoria. I've been so anxious for the hearings to wrap up so I could come meet you and your husband."

Victoria reached out and took her hands, not flinching at the coolness of the prosthesis. "Well, thank God they exonerated all of you. Ridiculous, wanting to imprison the experts who stopped those monsters. Let's hope that the special elections bring us the leadership we deserve. I hear people floating the name of your friend General Navarro as a possible candidate."

Elena gave a wry laugh. "We'll see. America and Russia aren't big fans of his, of course. I personally think he'd be great, but his wife and daughters may not want all the additional attention."

"Perhaps not. So come on inside, please. It's a bit nippy out, and I've got a delicious *chilatole* stew bubbling on the stove."

The three newcomers stepped through the doorway and into the comforts of home.

In the distance, a hazy yet sinister reminder loomed with muted menace over Zongolica:

The dormant volcano Orizaba, cloaked with dazzling snow.

A hint of smoke was curling from its summit.

END

CHECK OUT OTHER GREAT
KAIJU NOVELS

ATOMIC REX
by Matthew Dennion

The war is over, humanity has lost, and the Kaiju rule the earth.

Three years have passed since the US government attempted to use giant mechs to fight off an incursion of kaiju. The eight most powerful kaiju have carved up North America into their respective territories and their mutant offspring also roam the continent. The remnants of humanity are gathered in a remote settlement with Steel Samurai, the last of the remaining mechs, as their only protection. The mech is piloted by Captain Chris Myers who realizes that humanity will not survive if they stay at the settlement. In order to preserve the human race, he leaves the settlement unprotected as he engages on a desperate plan to draw the eight kaiju into each other's territories. His hope is that the kaiju will destroy each other. Chris will encounter horrors including the amorphous Amebos, Tortiraus the Giant turtle , and the nuclear powered mutant dinosaur Atomic Rex!

KAIJU DEADFALL
by JE Gurley

Death from space. The first meteor landed in the Pacific Ocean near San Francisco, causing an earthquake and a tsunami. The second wiped out a small Indiana city. The third struck the deserts of Nevada. When gigantic monsters- Ishom, Girra, and Nusku- emerge from the impact craters, the world faces a threat unlike any it had ever known - Kaiju . NASA catastrophist Gate Rutherford and Special Ops Captain Aiden Walker must find a way to stop the creatures before they destroy every major city in America..

CHECK OUT OTHER GREAT KAIJU NOVELS

KAIJU SPAWN
by David Robbins
& Eric S Brown

Wally didn't believe it was really the end of the world until he saw the Kaiju with his own eyes. The great beasts rose from the Earth's oceans, laying waste to civilization. Now Wally must fight his way across the Kaiju ravaged wasteland of modern day America in search of his daughter. He is the only hope she has left . . . and the clock is ticking.

From authors David Robbins (Endworld) and Eric S Brown (Kaiju Apocalypse), Kaiju Spawn is an action packed, horror tale of desperate determination and the battle to overcome impossible odds.

KUA MAU
by Mark Onspaugh

The Spider Islands. A mysterious ship has completed a treacherous journey to this hidden island chain. Their mission: to capture the legendary monster, Kua'Mau. Thinking they are successful, they sail back to the United States, where the terrifying creature will be displayed at a new luxury casino in Las Vegas. But the crew has made a horrible mistake - they did not trap Kua'Mau, they took her offspring. Now hot on their heels comes a living nightmare, a two hundred foot, one hundred ton tentacled horror, Kua'Mau, Kaiju Mother of Wrath, who will stop at nothing to safeguard her young. As she tears across California heading towards Vegas, she leaves a monumental body-count in her wake, and not even the U. S. military or private black ops can stop this city-crushing, havoc-wreaking monstrous mother of all Kaiju as she seeks her revenge.

 **SEVERED**PRESS

 facebook.com/severedpress
 twitter.com/severedpress

CHECK OUT OTHER GREAT KAIJU NOVELS

MURDER WORLD | KAIJU DAWN
by Jason Cordova
& Eric S Brown

Captain Vincente Huerta and the crew of the Fancy have been hired to retrieve a valuable item from a downed research vessel at the edge of the enemy's space.
It was going to be an easy payday.
But what Captain Huerta and the men, women and alien under his command didn't know was that they were being sent to the most dangerous planet in the galaxy.
Something large, ancient and most assuredly evil resides on the planet of Gorgon IV. Something so terrifying that man could barely fathom it with his puny mind. Captain Huerta must use every trick in the book, and possibly write an entirely new one, if he wants to escape Murder World.

KAIJU ARMAGEDDON
by Eric S. Brown

The attacks began without warning. Civilian and Military vessels alike simply vanished upon the waves. Crypto-zoologist Jerry Bryson found himself swept up into the chaos as the world discovered that the legendary beasts known as Kaiju are very real. Armies of the great beasts arose from the oceans and burrowed their way free of the Earth to declare war upon mankind. Now Dr. Bryson may be the human race's last hope in stopping the Kaiju from bringing civilization to its knees.
This is not some far distant future. This is not some alien world. This is the Earth, here and now, as we know it today, faced with the greatest threat its ever known. The Kaiju Armageddon has begun.

CHECK OUT OTHER GREAT KAIJU NOVELS

KAIJU WINTER
by Jake Bible

The Yellowstone super volcano has begun to erupt, sending North America into chaos and the rest of the world into panic. People are dangerous and desperate to escape the oncoming mega-eruption, knowing it will plunge the continent, and the world, into a perpetual ashen winter. But no matter how ready humanity is, nothing can prepare them for what comes out of the ash: Kaiju!

RAIJU
by K.H. Koehler

His home destroyed by a rampaging kaiju, Kevin Takahashi and his father relocate to New York City where Kevin hopes the nightmare is over. Soon after his arrival in the Big Apple, a new kaiju emerges. Qilin is so powerful that even the U.S. Military may be unable to contain or destroy the monster. But Kevin is more than a ragged refugee from the now defunct city of San Francisco. He's also a Keeper who can summon ancient, demonic god-beasts to do battle for him, and his creature to call is Raiju, the oldest of the ancient Kami. Kevin has only a short time to save the city of New York. Because Raiju and Qilin are about to clash, and after the dust settles, there may be no home left for any of them!

www.ingramcontent.com/pod-product-compliance
Lightning Source LLC
Chambersburg PA
CBHW051947170626
46808CB00007B/2524